THE STORY OF THE WONDERFUL WHITE FLOWER (page 101)

POLLY
OF THE HOSPITAL STAFF

BY

EMMA C. DOWD

WITH ILLUSTRATIONS

BOSTON AND NEW YORK
HOUGHTON MIFFLIN COMPANY
The Riverside Press Cambridge
1912

Published March 1912

TO
THE MOTHER
OF
"POLLY"

CONTENTS

ILLUSTRATIONS

From drawings by Irma Dérèmeaux

POLLY OF THE HOSPITAL STAFF

CHAPTER I

THE CHERRY-PUDDING STORY

THE June breeze hurried up from the harbor to the big house on the hill, and fluttered playfully past the window vines into the children's convalescent ward. It was a common saying at the hospital that the tidal breeze always reached the children's ward first. Sometimes the little people were waiting for it, ready with their welcome; but to-day there were none to laugh a greeting. The room was very quiet. The occupants of the little white cots had slept unusually long, and the few that had awakened from their afternoon naps were still too drowsy to be astir. Besides, Polly was not there, and the ward was never the same without Polly.

As the young nurse in charge passed noise-

1

lessly between the rows of beds, a small hand pulled at her apron.

"Ain't it 'most time for Polly to come?"

"Yes, I think she will be back pretty soon now." Miss Lucy smiled down into the wistful little face.

"I want Polly to tell me a story," Elsie went on, with a bit of a whine; "my hip aches so bad."

"Does it feel worse to-day?" asked the nurse sympathetically.

"No ; I guess not," answered the little girl, glad of a listener. "It aches all the time, 'cept when I'm asleep or Polly's tellin' stories."

"I know," and Miss Lucy's face grew grave. "We shall miss Polly."

"When's she goin' home?" The blue eyes went suddenly anxious.

"Oh, not until next week!" was the cheerful response. "There'll be time for plenty of stories before then."

"A-h-h!" wailed little French Aimée, from the opposite cot. "Pollee go?"

"Why, yes," smiled Miss Lucy, with a quick turn. "Polly is almost well, and well

2

little girls don't stay at the hospital, you know. Pretty soon you will go home, too."

The nurse passed on, but Aimée's face remained clouded. Next week —no Pollee!

Other ears besides Aimée's had overheard the news about Polly. Maggie O'Donnell and Otto Kriloff stared at each other in dismay. Why, Polly had been there long before they came! It had never occurred to them that Polly could leave.

When Miss Lucy reached Maggie's bed, the little girl was softly crying.

"I — don't — want — Polly to go!" she sobbed.

"Dear me! dear me!" exclaimed the nurse, "this will never do!" Then, listening, she whispered, "Hark! Who is that skipping along the hall?"

At the instant, the door opened, and a little girl, her brown eyes shining with pleasure, her cheeks pink as the poppies on the front lawn, and her yellow curls all tossed and tumbled by the wind, whirled into the ward.

"Oh, Polly!" passed, a breath of joy, from lip to lip.

"I've had a lovelicious time!" she began.

3

"We went 'way down to Rockmoor! — Did you ever ride in an auto, Miss Lucy?"

The nurse nodded happily. It was good to have Polly back.

"Seems's if you'd never come!" broke out Elsie Meyer. "I've been waitin' an' waitin' for a story."

"I'll have my things off in a minute," responded Polly, "and you'll say my story is worth waiting for."

"A new one?"

"Brand-new!"

"Where'd you get it?"

"A lady told me — a lady Dr. Dudley took me to see. It's a 'Cherry-Pudding Story.' — Oh, you just wait till I put my coat and hat away, and change my dress!" Polly danced off, the young nurse following with a soft sigh. What should she do without this little sunshine-maker!

The ward was wide awake when Polly returned. The few that were far enough along to be up and dressed had left their cots, and were grouped around Elsie Meyer's bed, each solicitous for the closest seat to the story-teller.

4

"ONCE UPON A TIME," SHE BEGAN

"Everybody ready?" questioned Polly, settling herself comfortably in the little rocker. Then she popped up. "You need this chair, Leonora, more than I do;" and before the lame girl had time to protest the exchange had been made.

"Polly, talk loud, so I can hear!" piped up a shrill voice in the farther corner of the ward.

"Sure I will, Linus," was the cheery response. "You must n't miss a word of the 'Cherry-Pudding story.'"

"Once upon a time," she began, in the beautiful old way that all fanciful stories should begin; and not the breath of a rustle broke the sound of her gentle voice, while she narrated the fortunes of the young king who loved stories so much that he decided to wed only the girl that would write him a fresh one every day.

As the little people followed the outcome of the royal edict, their interest grew intense, for Polly was a real story-teller, sweeping her listeners along with the narrative until all else was forgotten.

When, after long despairing days, young

5

King Cerise found his future queen in the very last girl, one who lived her stories instead of writing them, and was as charming and good as she was clever, the small folks became radiantly glad, and the tale drew to a happy end with the king and queen living beautiful stories and cherry puddings in every home all over the land.

Nobody spoke as Polly stopped. Then little Linus, away over in the corner, piped up: —

"I want some cherry pudding!"

That made them laugh, and set the tongues going.

"Aw, ye'll have ter wait till ye git home!" returned Cornelius O'Shaughnessy.

"Why will he? Why can't we all have some, Miss Lucy?"

The rest fairly held their breath at Elsie Meyer's boldness.

The nurse laughed. "Perhaps," she began slowly, — "mind, I don't say for sure, but only perhaps, — if you'll all live a brave, patient, cheerful story, with never a bit of a whine in it, from now until to-morrow noon, — well, who knows what may happen!"

6

"A cherry pudding may!" cried the irrepressible Elsie. "Oh, Miss Lucy, I won't whine or cry, no matter how bad you hurt my hip when you dress it — not the teentiest bit! See if I do!"

"Will Polly make up our stories for us?" queried Leonora Hewitt.

"Why, Miss Lucy has made one for all of us," laughed Polly. "We are to be brave and patient and not make a fuss about anything, and help everybody else to be happy — is n't that what you meant, Miss Lucy?"

"Oh," replied the little lame girl, "guess that 'll be a hard kind!"

"Beautiful stories are not often easy to live," smiled the young nurse; "but let's see which of us can live the best one."

"Polly will!" cried Maggie O'Donnell and Otto Kriloff together.

CHAPTER II

THE ELECTION OF POLLY

THE convalescent ward was finishing its noonday feast when Miss Hortensia Price appeared. Miss Hortensia Price was straight and tall, with sombre black eyes and thin, serious lips. Many of the children were greatly in awe of the dignified nurse; but Elsie Meyer was bold enough to announce: —

"We're livin' a cherry-pudding story!" And she beamed up from her ruby-colored plate.

"What?" scowled the visitor.

The tone was puzzled rather than harsh, yet Elsie shrank back in sudden abashment.

"Polly told us a story yesterday," explained Miss Lucy, the pink deepening on her delicate cheeks, "and it made the children want some cherry pudding for dinner. It is not rich," she added apologetically.

The elder nurse responded only with a

8

courteous "Oh!" and then remarked, "What I came down to say is this: I shall send you three cases from my ward at half-past two o'clock this afternoon."

"All right," was the cordial answer. "We shall be glad to welcome them to our little family."

"High Price is awful solemn to-day," whispered Maggie O'Donnell to Ethel Jones, as the door shut.

"High Price?" repeated Ethel, in a perplexed voice.

"Sh!" breathed the other. "She's 'High Price,' and Miss Lucy's 'Low Price,' 'cause she's so high and mighty and tall and everything, and Miss Lucy's kind o' short and little and so darling, and they ain't any relation either. I'm glad they ain't," she added decidedly. "I would n't have Miss Lucy related to her for *anything!*"

"Oh, no!" returned Ethel, comprehendingly, as she scraped her plate for a last morsel of pudding.

The three "cases," which appeared in the convalescent ward promptly at the hour named, proved to be two girls and a boy, —

Brida MacCarthy, Isabel Smith, and Moses Cohn. Polly did her share in routing the evident fears of the small strangers, their wide, anxious eyes showing that they dreaded what might lie ahead of them in these unknown quarters.

The wonderful giant story, which ended merrily, — as all of Polly's stories did end, — made Moses her valiant follower as long as he remained in the ward; the tender little slumber song, which Polly's mother had taught her, put the tiny Isabel to sleep; and the verses about the "Kit-Cat Luncheon" completely won the heart of Irish Brida.

"I got a kitty, too!" she confided. "Her name 's Popover, 'cause when the kitties was all little, an' runnin' round, an' playin', she'd pop right over on her back, jus' as funny! She 's all black concept a little spot o' white — oh, me kitty is the prettiest kitty in town!"

"How shall I ever get along without her!" sighed the young nurse, as she watched Polly flitting about like a sprite, comforting restless little patients, hushing, with her ready tact, quarrelsome tongues, and winning every heart by her gentle, loving ways. Oh, the ward would be lonely indeed without Polly May! None realized this more than Miss Lucy, unless it were Dr. Dudley, the cheery house physician, whom all the children adored.

As the day set for Polly's going came near and nearer, the mourning of the small convalescents increased, until the ward would have been in danger of continual tears if it had not been for Polly herself. She was gayer than ever, telling the funniest stories and singing the merriest songs, and making her little friends half forget that the good times were not going to last. The children never guessed that this was almost as much to help herself over the hard place as to cheer them. In fact, they believed that her unusual high spirits came of her being glad to leave the hospital. Even Miss Lucy couldn't quite understand it all. But Dr. Dudley knew; he had seen her face when she had been told that she was soon to go.

It was not strange that Polly should dread parting from the people with whom she had been so happy, for no mother or father or pleasant home was waiting for her, — only

11

Aunt Jane, in the cramped, dingy little tenement, — Aunt Jane and her six unruly girls
and boys. Polly did not permit herself to think
much about going away, however, and the
last evening found her cheerful still. Then
Elsie Meyer began her doleful suggestions.

"I wonder how often your Aunt Jane 'll
let you come and see us. P'r'aps she won't
let you come at all — oh, my! If she don't,
maybe we 'll never see you again!"

"Nonsense, Elsie! don't go to conjuring
up any such thing!" broke in Miss Lucy's
laughing voice. "Of course — why, Polly!"
For the little girl had been brought suddenly
face to face with an awful possibility, and her
courage had given way. She was sobbing on
the foot of Elsie's bed.

A low rap on the half-open door sent Miss
Lucy thither, and Polly heard Dr. Dudley
speak her name. A new terror took instant
possession of her heart. The Doctor had come
to take her home! She did not stop to reason.
Dropping to the floor, she crept softly under
the cot, from there to the next and the next.
Her course was straight to the door through
which the physician had entered, and by the

time he was halfway across the room she had wriggled herself clear of the last cot, and was over the sill and in the corridor, the twilight aiding her escape. Regaining her feet, she darted noiselessly down the long hall. At the head of the stairs she paused. On the floor below was a small alcove where she might hide. Making sure that no one was in sight, she sped down, but as she reached the lower step one of the nurses opened the door opposite.

"What are you doing down here, Polly May?"

The question was pleasant, but the answer was miserably halting.

"I — I — thought — I'd just — come —"

"Did Miss Price send you for anything?"

This time the child detected a ring of suspicion.

"Oh, no! I — I —"

"Well, you'd better go right back. It is too late to be running around for play. The halls must be kept quiet."

"Yes, Miss Bemont," responded Polly meekly, and turned to see Dr. Dudley at the head of the flight.

13

There was nothing to do but to go forward, which she did, with downcast eyes and a throbbing heart.

"Oh, here you are!" exclaimed the physician. "I've been looking for you. I thought you would like to take a ride up to Warringford. I shall be back before your bedtime, and Miss Lucy says — why, Thistledown! what is the matter?"

The revulsion had been too great, and, leaning against the Doctor's arm, Polly was softly sobbing.

The physician sat down on the stairs, and drew the fair little head to his shoulder. In a minute he knew it all, — the sudden fear that had assailed her, the creeping flight across the ward, and the baffled attempt at hiding. As he listened, his eyes grew grave and tender, for in the broken little confession he comprehended the child's unspoken abhorrence of the life she had left behind when she had come to the hospital five months before.

"I would n't worry about going back to Aunt Jane's," he said brightly. "You may be sure I shan't let her monopolize my little

14

Polly. Now, run along and get on your hat and coat, for the air is growing cool. We'll have a nice spin up to Warringford, and you'll sleep all the better for it."

Polly skipped away smiling, but presently was down in the office, — without her wraps.

"The children feel so bad to have me go," she said soberly, "I guess I'd better stay with them — seeing it's the last night." Her lip quivered.

"Selfish little pigs!" returned the Doctor. "They aren't willing anybody else shall have a taste of you."

Polly laughed. "Well, they want me to tell them a story, so I'd better, don't you think?"

"I suppose it's kinder to them than to go for a joy ride; but it's hard on me."

Dr. Dudley assumed a scowl of disapproval.

The child hesitated. "You know I'd rather go with you," she said sweetly; "but they —"

"I understand all about it, brave little woman," throwing an arm around the slender shoulders, "and I won't make it any

15

harder for you. Go and tell your story, and let it be a merry one. Remember, that's the Doctor's order! Good-night."

Polly threw him a kiss from the doorway, and then he heard her light footfalls on the stairs.

It was one of his few leisure hours, and he sat for a long time looking out on the quiet street, where his small motor car stood waiting. He had no inclination for a spin to Warringford now; he was thinking too deeply about the little girl who had held so large a share of his big heart since the day when he had first seen her, lying so white and still, with the life all but crushed out of her. It had not seemed possible then that she would ever again dance around like other children; yet here she was, without even the bit of a limp — and going home to-morrow! Home! He could imagine the kind of place it was, and he shook his head gravely over the picture. Twice in the first months of Polly's stay at the hospital her aunt had been to visit her; recently she had not appeared. He recollected her well,—a tall, lean woman, with unshapely garments, and a strident voice.

16

At eight o'clock Dr. Dudley cranked up his machine, and started away; but he did not go in the direction of Warringford. He turned down one of the narrow streets that led to Aunt Jane's home.

Meantime, up in the ward, Polly had been following the Doctor's directions until the children had laughed themselves happy.

"I did n't let on that I saw you scoot under the bed when the Doctor came," Elsie Meyer whispered to Polly, at the first chance. "Aimée saw you, an' Brida saw you, an' Francesca saw you; but we did n't say nothin' when Miss Lucy an' the Doctor was wonderin' where you could be. What made you go that way?"

"Come, Polly, say good-night," called the nurse.

And with a soft, "I'll tell you sometime, Elsie," she obeyed.

The next morning Polly went about the little helpful tasks that she had, one after another, taken upon herself, performing each with even more than her usual care, feeling a strange ache in her heart at the thought of its being the last time.

17

It was shortly after ten o'clock that Dr. Dudley appeared at the door.

"Polly!" he called.

She ran to him, but her answering smile was pathetic, for her lip quivered, as she said, "I'll be ready in a minute."

"You are ready now," he returned, and taking her hand in his led her out into the hall.

"I want you for a little while," was all he said, as they went downstairs together.

Polly was a bit surprised when she found that their destination was the great room where the "Board" was in session, but she could not be afraid with Dr. Dudley; so she smiled to all the gentlemen, and answered their questions in her soft, sweet voice, and behaved quite like the little lady that the physician had pictured to them.

Presently Dr. Dudley left her, while he talked in low tones with the white-haired man at the head of the long table. When he came back, he asked: —

"Polly, how should you like to stay here at the hospital all summer, and help Miss Lucy and me to take care of your little friends?"

18

The light that flashed into Polly's brown
eyes gave them the gleam of a sunny brook.
She clasped her small hands ecstatically,
crying, "O—o—h! it would be — super-
bon-donjical!"

The gentlemen laughed, the tall, white-
haired one until his shoulders shook. Then
he rapped on the table, and said something
about "Miss Polly May," to which the little
girl didn't pay much attention, and there
was a big chorus of ayes. After that Polly
bade them all good-bye, and went upstairs
with Dr. Dudley.

"Children, I have something to tell you,"
the physician announced.

Everybody was at once alert. A solemn
hush fell on the ward.

"What do you think?" he went on; —
"Polly May is a full-fledged member of the
hospital staff!"

Nobody spoke. Nobody even smiled but
Miss Lucy. Black eyes and brown eyes, blue
eyes and gray eyes stared uncomprehend-
ingly at the Doctor.

"You don't quite understand that, do
you?" he laughed. "Well, it means that

19

Polly is n't going home to her aunt. Polly is going to stay with you!''

Then what squeals and shouts and shrieks of joy from all over the ward!

little shop numbered 703; but with the glad thought that the "brown house" could not be far off she began to look for it.

Directly across her way was stretched a jumping rope, which, as she was about to step over, the girls at either end whirled up in front of her. To the astonishment of the mischievous tricksters, Polly skipped into time as adroitly as the most expert rope-jumper could have wished, and the giggling pair almost forgot their part. But they recovered themselves to give Polly a half-dozen skips. Then, clearing the rope with a graceful bound, she turned to one of the girls.

"Can you tell me, please, where Mrs. MacCarthy lives? — Brida MacCarthy's mother?"

With a second surprise on her freckled face, the child pointed to a fat, red-cheeked woman, who was cooling herself with a big palm-leaf fan, in a basement doorway just beyond.

"Thank you," was the polite response, and Polly descended the short flight of steps into the bricked area.

The woman looked up expectantly.

"I'm Polly May, of the hospital staff," the little girl announced modestly, "and Brida would like her kitten, please."

The smile on Mrs. MacCarthy's face expanded into a big, joyous laugh.

"Does she now? Moira! Katie! D'ye hear that? Brida's sint f'r her cat! Sure an' she moost be gittin' 'long rale well! An' ye're from th' hospital! Moira! where's yer manners? Fetch th' little lady a chair! Katie, git a mug o' wather an' wan o' thim big crackers. Don't ye know how to trate comp'ny?"

In a minute Polly was seated, a china mug of water in one hand, and a crisp soda biscuit in the other, while the MacCarthy family circled around her, eager for news from the beloved Brida. There were only encouraging accounts to give of the little girl with the broken ankle; but they led to so many questions that Polly began to wonder how she should ever escape from these friendly people, when Popover herself solved the question.

The pretty black kitten suddenly appeared

at the visitor's side, and at the first caressing word from Polly jumped into her lap.

"D' ye see that?" cried the delighted mother, and in the momentary excitement Polly arose and said that she must go.

Brida's sisters and small brother accompanied her for two blocks up the street, and then, with numerous good-byes, they left her to her long, wearisome walk.

She had not gone far before she realized that the warm little animal was more of a burden than she had counted on, exhausted as she was already with her unusual exercise; but she kept up courageously, even making little spurts of speed as she would wonder if Miss Lucy were becoming anxious about her. After awhile, however, instead of hurrying, she was obliged to stop now and then on a corner, to catch the breeze coming up from the sea, for she felt strangely faint. When she finally trudged up Hospital Hill, the air grew cool all at once, and she quite forgot herself for thinking of Brida and Miss Lucy.

At the door of the ward she paused for a peep. The nurse was not in sight. A few of the children were gathered at the windows with books and pictures; several were on the floor playing quiet games. So softly did she step that nobody knew she was there until she was well in the room. Then, spying both her and the kitten, there was a shout and a rush.

"No, you can't have her yet!" cried Polly, as small hands were outstretched to lift the now uneasy burden from her arms. "Brida has first right, because it's her kitten."

"Oh, Popover!" squealed the little owner delightedly, snuggling the furry creature to her cheek.

"Where's Miss Lucy?" demanded Polly, waiving the children's eager questions.

"Oh, they sent to have her come somewhere!" answered Ethel Jones. "She went in an awful hurry, and said prob'ly she'd be back pretty soon; but she has n't come yet."

"She let Leonora be monitor," put in Elsie Meyer. "I guess she'd 'a' let me, if I'd been up."

"I wish she would come," said Polly anxiously, "for I want to surprise her with Popover — it's Miss Lucy's birthday, you know."

"Somebody's coming now," and Cornelius O'Shaughnessy bent his head to listen. "'T ain't her step," he decided disappointedly, and the next moment the tall form of Miss Hortensia Price was seen in the doorway.

"Quick! keep her out o' sight!" whispered Polly, pushing Popover's little black head down under the sheet.

The stately young woman walked the length of the room without a word, and calmly sat down at the small table where Miss Lucy was accustomed to prepare her medicines and to make such notes as were needful.

As Miss Price took up the little memorandum book and began to look it over, Polly's heart almost stood still with consternation. She had come to stay! Polly knew the signs. Such sudden shifts were common enough in the hospital, but only twice, during Polly's stay, had they occurred in the convalescent ward, and Miss Lucy had been in charge for so long now that she had ceased giving herself any worry over a possible change.

For a moment the little girl stood hesitant; then the sight of Brida, white and scared on her pillow, roused her to quick thought. If she could only smuggle Popover down into Dr. Dudley's office before she was discovered! Instinct told her that "High Price" would never tolerate a kitten in the ward. She took one step forward.

"Me-ew!" sounded faintly from Brida's cot.

The nurse raised her head, listened inquiringly, and then resumed her work of examining the patients' records.

Polly stole nearer the bed.

"Me-ew!" came again, louder than before. This time there was no mistaking its locality.

Miss Price sprang from her chair, and strode straight to where Brida lay trembling. Popover's insistence for more air and a free outlook was causing the coverlet to rise and fall in a startling way.

"How came that cat here?" demanded the nurse, pulling aside the bedclothing.

"I brought her," answered Polly. "She's Brida's kitty, and we were going to give Miss Lucy a birthday surprise."

30

A faint smile flickered on the young woman's face. Then she made a grab at the now frightened kitten; but the little creature slipped from her hand, and jumping to the floor darted towards the hall.

"Oh, me darlin' kitty!" wailed Brida. "She'll be losted! Oh, Polly, ketch her!"

Polly, however, was already flying in pursuit of the terrified cat.

"Shut that door!" called the mistress of the ward, as the eager children rushed after. "And stay inside, all of you!"

Cornelius O'Shaughnessy reluctantly obeyed the first order, and the rest trailed back in disappointment. So exciting a race was not an everyday occurrence.

Polly, too far away to heed either command, was alarmed lest Popover might manage to escape from the building, in which case there would be small chance of catching her. On and on the little cat led her, giving no ear to the coaxing, "Kitty, Kitty, Kitty!" which she was constantly calling. Around and around the big halls, up this flight of stairs and down that, into room after room whose doors stood enticingly open, raced Popover and Polly, while nurses and physicians that chanced their way stared and laughed at the astonishing sight.

Just as the kitten reached the foot of the first-floor staircase, with her pursuer close behind, the front door opened, and Popover darted towards the passage of escape.

"Oh, shut the door quick! Catch her! Catch her! Don't let her get out!"

This most unexpected command, in Polly's voice, Dr. Dudley endeavored to obey. He did succeed in slamming the door in front of pussy, though at the risk of nipping her little black nose; but when he stooped to snatch her she slipped between his feet, and dashed into his office. Polly flew after, and the door went together just as the Doctor reached it.

"Rather an unusual reception this is," he twinkled, as Polly let him in, a minute later. "Frighten me out of my wits by screaming at me to catch a wild animal, and then, when I've done my best, shut the door of my office right in my face! What do you mean by such extraordinary conduct, Miss Polly May?" The physician shook a threatening finger at the flushed and laughing little girl.

"You don't look very scared," she giggled; and then as he dropped into his lounging-chair she slipped into her favorite position, atilt on its arm, and leaned confidingly against him.

"Oh, I've had such a time with that kitten!" she sighed, smiling across at the little creature, now curled up contentedly on the Doctor's fur rug.

"I take it, by the way you are breathing, that you and the cat have been having a race."

"All over everywhere," answered Polly, "till I thought I'd never catch her. You see she was going to be a birthday surprise to Miss Lucy, and High Price went and spoiled it all."

The story of the afternoon was narrated in Polly's most vivid style.

"Isn't it queer that High Price should come just then?" she sighed. "I don't like her; do you?"

"She is an excellent young woman and a good nurse," Dr. Dudley returned.

"Well, I don't want her for my nurse," Polly maintained soberly.

33

"Still, if you were very sick," smiled the Doctor, "I could not hope for better care than she would give you."

"Oh, if I were awfully sick, and out of my head, maybe High Price would do; but if I knew anything I should want Miss Lucy." And Polly's curls waved in emphasis.

Dr. Dudley chuckled responsively.

"I don't think you appreciate Miss Lucy," Polly continued.

The Doctor's eyebrows went up. "Don't I?" he returned meekly.

"You don't act as if you did," Polly sighed; "and I want you to, for she's so sweet and little and — cuddly, you know. You could n't call High Price cuddly; could you?"

"It is n't a term I should apply to her," agreed the Doctor, with the hint of a smile.

"Miss Lucy would have liked Popover. It's too bad! I don't see how we're ever going to get along without Miss Lucy, 'specially at bedtime."

"What does she do then?"

"Oh, we tell stories! — at least, I do, and sometimes she does, and generally we sing —

real soft, you know, so it won't disturb anybody. Then she says a little prayer, and we
go to bed. Dear me, how we shall miss her!
Why, the other night, when Aimée's arm
ached, Miss Lucy took her right in her lap,
and rocked her to sleep! And when little Isabel cries for her mamma, Miss Lucy's just
as nice to her, and cuddles her up so sweet!
This is the way High Price will do: she'll say,
'Is-a-bel'" (and Polly's tone was in almost
exact imitation of the nurse's measured ac-
cent), "'lie still and go to sleep! The ward
must be kept quiet.'"

Dr. Dudley laughed. Then he said
gravely: —

"Do you think that is really fair — to ac-
cuse Miss Price of what she may never do?
Besides, Polly, it is n't quite respectful."

"No, I suppose it is n't," the little girl admitted. "Excuse me, please. But I wish you
could know the difference between High
Price and Low Price."

The Doctor's eyes twinkled; but Polly, all
unseeing, went on: —

"How soon do you think Miss Lucy'll
come back? Where is she now?"

"She has been assigned to one of the wo-men's wards. It is uncertain when she will be changed again."

"Well, I s'pose we'll have to stand it," sighed Polly philosophically. "Why, Pop-over!" for the kitten had come up unnoticed, and now jumped to the Doctor's knee. "Is n't she cute? Brida thinks lots of her — there!" she broke out compunctiously, "I forgot all about Brida, and she does n't know what's become of her! I must run up and tell her. Will it be very much trouble to keep her here till to-morrow? Then I'll carry her home."

"Suppose we take her home in the auto, after tea?"

"Oh, lovely!"

Dr. Dudley was looking at his watch.

"Is it 'most tea-time?" Polly inquired.

"They are probably all through up in the convalescent ward," he laughed. "You'd better come into the dining-room and have supper with me."

"Oh, thank you; that will be nice! I'll run up and tell Brida, and then I'll come."

CHAPTER IV

DAVID

D R. DUDLEY had been the rounds of the convalescent ward, to see how his patients were progressing. Now he had paused at the small table by the window, where Polly was waiting to carry some medicine to Linus Hardy.

As she took the glass from Miss Price's hand, and started away, she heard the physician say, "Can I have Polly for a few minutes?"

"Certainly, Dr. Dudley," was the reply; and Polly returned wondering what was wanted of her.

"There is a boy upstairs who is getting discouraged," the Doctor began, as they went through the hall, hand in hand, "and I think, perhaps, you can cheer him up a little."

"Is he a big boy or a little boy?" asked Polly anxiously.

37

"I should say, about six months bigger than you," the Doctor laughed. "He is n't anybody you will be afraid of, Thistledown; but he is a very nice boy. His mother is just recovering from a severe illness, so she has n't been able to come to see him yet, and he feels pretty lonely."

"I wish he were down in our ward," returned Polly, — "that is," she amended, "if Miss Lucy were only there."

"I shall have him transferred as soon as he is well enough," the Doctor assured her. And then they were at the entrance of the children's ward.

Away to the farther end of the room Dr. Dudley went, and Polly followed. Some of the patients looked curiously at her as she passed, for the news of her recent accession to the staff had spread through the hospital, and nearly everybody was eager for a sight of her.

Polly was thinking only of the boy whom she had come to see; and when, at last, the Doctor stopped and turned towards her, she glanced shyly at the lad on the pillow.

"David," began Dr. Dudley, "this is Miss

38

Polly May, the chief story-teller of the convalescent ward. And, Polly, allow me to present Master David Collins, who had a race, a week or two ago, with a runaway horse, and who was foolish enough to let the horse beat."

The Doctor's eyes were twinkling, and Polly let go a giggle; so the boy ventured to laugh. A weak little laugh it was; but it helped to start the acquaintance pleasantly, which was just what Dr. Dudley wanted.

"You can have exactly ten minutes to do all your talking in," was the physician's parting sally; "so you'd better hurry."

Polly's eyes and David's met in smiling appreciation.

"He says such funny things," praised Polly.

"Yes," agreed David.

Polly did n't quite know how to begin to cheer the lad up. Her tender heart was stirred to unusual sympathy, as she gazed into the pitifully drawn little face, with its big doll-blue eyes. She must surely say something to make David happier — and the minutes

39

were going fast. After all, it was David that
was first to speak again.

"Do you like stories?" he asked.

"Oh, I just love them!"

"So do I. You must know a great many.
The Doctor said you told them to the children. I wish there was time for you to tell
me one."

"I 'm afraid there is n't to-day," responded Polly; "but maybe I can stay
longer when I come again."

"I hope so," returned David politely.
"My mother read me a story the evening
before I was hurt. It was about a king and
queen that lived beautiful stories, and I was
going to live such a brave, splendid one
every day — and then the horse knocked me
down! Such a lot of miserable stories as
I 've lived since I came here, not much like
the ones I 'd planned! But to-day's will be
better, because you 'll be in it," he ended
brightly.

Polly's eyes had been growing rounder
and rounder with surprise and delight.

"Oh! was it a Cherry-Pudding Story?"
she asked eagerly.

40

"Why, have you read it?" and the little white face actually grew pink. "My aunt wrote it, and sent us a paper that had it in!"

"Why — ee!" cried Polly. "Is n't that funny! And we've been trying to live nice stories, too — all of us, up in the ward! Miss Lucy said we'd see which could live the best one. A lady told me the story. And your aunt really made it all up?"

"Yes; she writes lots of stories," smiled David. "Then she sends them to mamma and me when they're printed."

"How splendid!" beamed Polly. "When you get well enough to come down in our ward, you can tell us some, can't you?"

The boy's face saddened. "I guess I can't ever come," he said.

"Why not?"

"Because I was hurt so badly. I don't think I'm going to get well."

"Oh, yes, you will!" asserted Polly. "Of course Dr. Dudley will cure you! Goodness! you ought to have seen how I was all smashed up! But Dr. Dudley cured me — he can cure anybody!"

"He can?" echoed David, a little doubtfully. "How 'd you get hurt? Were you run over?"

"Yes, by a building," Polly laughed. "Only it did n't run; it fell. I was 'way up on the third floor, and all of a sudden it went — just like that!" Polly's little hands dropped flat in her lap. "I heard a great noise, and felt myself going, and I remember I clutched hold of Uncle Gregory. Then I did n't know another thing till I woke up over in that corner. See that bed with the dark-haired little girl in it, the third from the end? That was my cot."

"Was your leg broken?" asked David, in a most interested tone.

"Yes, my leg was broken, and my hip was *discolated*" (Polly sometimes twisted her long words a little), "and my ankle was hurt, and two ribs, and, oh, lots of things! Doctor says now that he really did n't think I'd ever walk again — I mean, without crutches."

"And you're not lame a bit?" David returned incredulously.

"Not a mite, not the least mite!" Polly assured him.

"Then perhaps I shall get well," the boy began brightly.

"Of course you will!" broke in Dr. Dudley's happy voice.

He put his hand on the lad's wrist, and stood for a moment, noting his pulse.

"It does n't seem to hurt you to have visitors," he smiled; "but they must n't stay too long. Say good-bye, Polly."

"Will you bring her again to-morrow?" invited David timidly. "And let her stay long enough to tell me a story?"

"I should n't wonder," the Doctor promised. And they left the boy smiling as he had not smiled since he had been in the hospital.

After that, Polly went every day to see David, until, one morning, Dr. Dudley told her that he was not quite well enough to have a visitor. She had come to look forward to her quiet talks with the blue-eyed lad as the happiest portion of the whole day, for Miss Hortensia Price still stayed in the convalescent ward, and the Doctor had been too busy lately to take her out in his automobile. Elsie and Brida and Aimée and the

43

rest were all good comrades, yet none of them possessed David's powers of quick comprehension. Often Polly had to explain things to them; David always kept up with her thought — there was the difference. And David, notwithstanding his present proneness to discouragement, was a most winsome boy.

So the first day that she was not allowed to make her customary visit seemed a long day indeed, and eagerly she awaited the next morning. But several days passed before she again saw David. Then it was but for a very few minutes, and he was so wan and weak that she went away feeling sorrowful and anxious. Yet Dr. Dudley told her that she had done his patient good. That was a slight comfort.

The next day, and the next, the lad was again too ill for company, and a few sentences which Polly overheard filled her with foreboding. She was putting fresh sheets on one of the cots — a task which she had learned to do well — when she caught David's name.

"His heart is very weak," one of the upstairs nurses was saying to Miss Price. "He can't stand many more such sinking spells. Dr. Dudley has given orders to be called at once, day or night, if he should have another."

Here the voice dropped, and Polly could not catch the words; but she had heard enough. The sheet went on crookedly. Polly did not know it, her eyes were so blurred with tears. She kept the sorry news to herself, and all day long the children wondered what made Polly so sober.

If she could have seen Dr. Dudley she would have asked him about David; but for several days she caught only passing glimpses of him, when he was too busy to be questioned. The little girl grew more and more anxious, but kept hoping that because she heard nothing David must be better.

It was during the short absence of Miss Price, one afternoon, that Elsie Meyer complained of the disagreeable liniment on her hip.

"It's just horrid! I can't stand it a minute longer!" she fretted. "Say, Polly, I wish

45

you'd spray some of that nice-smellin' stuff around — what do you call it?''

"The resodarizer, I guess you mean," responded Polly, with more glibness than accuracy.

"Yes, that's it," Elsie returned. "Hurry up and use it, before High Price gets back!''

"Perhaps I'd better wait and ask her," she hesitated.

"No, don't! Miss Lucy always lets you take it," Elsie urged.

"Yes, I know," doubtfully. Then she went to the shelf in the dressing-room, where the atomizer box stood.

"There is n't a drop in it," she said, holding the bottle to the light. "Miss Lucy must have forgotten to fill it after I used it last time." Then, spying a small phial on the shelf, close to where the box had been, "Oh, I guess she left it for me to fill!" And, unscrewing the chunky little bottle from the spraying apparatus, she soon had it half full.

Elsie smiled in blissful anticipation of the refreshing perfume, but as the spray fell near her she greeted it with a torrent of cries.

"Ugh, ugh! O-o-h! take it away!"

Then Polly, too, puckered her face in disgust. "Why, I must have put —"

"What are you doing with that atomizer?" interrupted Miss Price's voice. "How came kerosene oil in here? Have you been spraying it around?"

"I did n't know it was kerosene," answered Polly meekly. "I s'posed it was the resodarizer —"

"Deodorizer, child!"

"Oh, yes, I get it twisted! It 's that kind that smells so nice."

Miss Price gave a little laugh. "Well, this does n't smell nice."

"I 'm sorry," mourned Polly. "I don't see how a kerosene bottle came up there — oh, I know! Miss Lucy was putting some on her watch, the other day, and she was called off — I remember! She must have left it there."

"But the bottle is labeled," Miss Price replied, fetching it from the table where Polly had set it down. "Can't you read?"

"Of course I can!" she answered, a little indignant at the question. "I guess I was thinking of — something else," she ended.

"David" had been on her tongue, but she kept the name back.

"Don't you know that you should always have your mind on what you do? It is a mercy that you did not get hold of anything worse."

"I could n't," Polly protested. "The poisons and all such things are up in the medicine closet, and that's always locked."

"You have been allowed too much liberty," Miss Price went on. "Hereafter remember that you are not to touch a bottle of any description. But, then," she added, half to herself, but which came plainly to Polly's ear, "there is no need of such an order while I am in charge. I shall see that none are left within reach."

The child's eyes flashed. This clear implication of the one she adored set loose her temper, and she burst out passionately: —

"Miss Lucy always does everything just right, and I think it 's mean of you to hint that she does n't!"

Miss Price looked steadily at Polly, the color wavering on her cheeks; then she said, with more than her usual gentleness: —

48

"Polly, I am sorry, but I think I shall have to punish you. You may go and sit in that wooden chair over there, with your back to the window. Do not stir or speak until I give you permission."

Polly walked straight to the seat designated, but there was no meekness in her obedience. She carried her head defiantly, and her face was hot with anger. To think that "High Price" should dare to find fault with Miss Lucy! That rankled in her loyal little heart.

CHAPTER V

A STRAIN of music floated up from the street, and the children that were able to be on their feet rushed for the windows.

"It's a band wagon!" cried Ethel.

"Two!" amended Moses. "Say, Miss Price, can't Polly just come and look at 'em?"

"No," was the quiet answer, while Cornelius O'Shaughnessy made faces at the young woman's back.

But Polly was not missing as much as the children feared. At first her mind was in too great a tumult for her to care for band wagons. Then, as the music soothed her excited nerves and drew her thoughts into pleasanter paths, she pictured the great wagons, and the performers in scarlet and gold, as she had seen them scores of times, and she seemed to watch their progress under the

50

arch of elms as perfectly as if she were not in the middle of the room with her eyes shut.

The music grew faint and fainter, and was finally lost in the noise of the street. The children returned to their various occupations, giving Polly furtive tokens of sympathy on their way back. Leonora squeezed her hand; Cornelius patted her shoulder; Moses gently pulled a curl — one of his friendly amusements; and Brida, who was now about on crutches, stooped to kiss her cheek.

"Brida, do not talk to Polly!"

The sudden command startled the child almost into tripping.

"I was n't talkin'!" she protested. "I was only kissin' her."

"Well, come away from her — clear away," for the little girl was not making very quick time.

"I'm comin' 's fas' 's I can!" she pouted. "I can't *run* on these old crutches — so there!"

Polly almost giggled aloud at Brida's daring, but promptly subsided into a safe look of gravity. It was pleasant to feel sure of her

51

friends. She was still thinking in this vein when a rap on the half-closed door was at once followed by the frightened face of one of the upstairs young nurses.

"Oh, Polly!" she cried, at sight of her, "run quick, and catch Dr. Dudley for David! He's out there cranking up, and I can't —"

But Polly had shot past her, and was already on the stairs.

The physician was starting his car, as she gained the front entrance.

"Doctor! Doctor! Oh, Doctor!" she screamed, dashing down steps and walk at a reckless speed; but he did not look round, and her voice was lost in the noise of the machine.

Her feet never slackened. Straight on she flew, like a real thistledown, her fair curls streaming on the wind, her eyes big with a vague terror. As the Doctor sped farther and farther away from her, she ceased calling, realizing that she must reach him in some other way.

The second house below the hospital was Colonel Gresham's. The Colonel himself was stepping into his light buggy, to give Lone Star, his favorite trotter, a little exercise, when Polly rushed up.

"Oh, please, sir!" she panted, "will you catch Dr. Dudley? — They want him at the hospital — and I could n't make him hear! He 's right ahead — in his auto — the dark green one! David will die if he don't come!"

For answer, Polly was whirled into the carriage, and before she could recover her breath Lone Star was making as good time as he had ever made in his short but famous life.

"Whew! the Colonel is going some!" — "Who 's that pretty little kid with him?" — "Don't he leg it, though!" These and kindred observations were elicited all the way down the street, men stopping to see the well-known horse go by, and children scurrying across his track.

But the Doctor seemed bent on leading his pursuers a lengthy chase, for no sooner had they gained on him sufficiently to set Polly's heart dancing with hope than he suddenly increased his speed, at once putting a greater distance between them. Then, slowing for an instant, he vanished round a distant corner.

"Zounds!" muttered the Colonel.

"He turned right opposite that white birch!" cried Polly.

"Sure?"

"Yes; I was keeping watch."

So was the Colonel; but he had not noticed the tree.

Polly's assurance held enough decision to satisfy the driver, and he took the turn she had indicated, where the glint of the weeping white birch on the opposite side of the street had caught her observant eye. But on the cross-road no dark green auto was in sight.

As they came to the first street on the right, however, a solitary car met their eager eyes.

Polly looked her delight, as they swept round the corner and along the hard, clear stretch. The flicker of a smile was on the Colonel's rugged face.

"Doc—tor! Doctor Dud—ley!" called Polly.

The physician turned his head.

"Oh, don't stop!" she entreated, for he

was slowing up, as they came alongside. "Please go right back — quick! David's worse!"

One astonished glance, and he comprehended, and obeyed. Colonel Gresham gave him room for the turn. Then, with a graceful gesture of farewell, and, "I thank you!" he whizzed past them and out of sight.

"Oh, I hope he'll get there in time!" sighed Polly.

"I think he will," the Colonel nodded. "He looks it."

"I don't want David to die; he's such a nice boy."

Lone Star was taking the road easily, after his spurt of speed. The lines lay loosely on the Colonel's knee.

"Is this David some relative of yours?" he asked.

"Oh, no, sir! I've only known him a few weeks, since he was knocked down by a runaway horse, and hurt so badly. He's David Collins, and I'm Polly May. Dr. Dudley took me up to see him, because he needed cheering up; but now he has bad turns with his heart, and I can't go. He's a lovely boy.

55

It was so good of you to take me to catch the Doctor — I don't know what I should have done if you had n't! And did n't your horse go fast! I never saw a horse go so fast before. I think he's beautiful; don't you?"

"I like him." The Colonel smiled down into Polly's eyes quite as if they were old friends. "Suppose I take you for a little longer drive — would your friends mind?"

"Oh, thank you!" Polly began, "I'd love it!" Then she stopped, with sudden recollection. "I guess I can't, though — I'd forgotten all about it! — I must go back, and finish being punished."

Colonel Gresham laughed outright, so Polly laughed too.

"I made an awful mistake," she explained; "I sprayed some kerosene all around, instead of de-sodarizer."

The Colonel was grave for a polite moment. Then, "And you did n't smell it?" he laughed.

"Not till Elsie yelled at me to stop. I don't see why I did n't."

"But it seems hardly fair to punish one for a mistake."

56

"Well," confessed Polly, "that was n't all. I got mad, and I guess I was pretty saucy to High Price. She said something about Miss Lucy that I did n't like, and I told her what I thought — I just had to! So she sent me to sit in a chair till she said to get up. Then when the nurse came for me to catch Dr. Dudley, I was so scared about David that I ran right off, without even asking permission — I don't know what she will do to me now! But you can't stop for anything when folks are 'most dying, can you?"

"I should say not," the Colonel replied. "I reckon she won't treat you very badly."

"I don't care what she does, if David only gets well. But, oh, how can David's mother stand it, if he does n't! She's sick, you know, so she could n't come to see him — he's all she's got, and such a dear boy! He works to earn money for her when he's well, sells papers, and everything. I guess they're rather poor; but perhaps I ought n't to talk about that. Please don't tell anybody I said it, 'cause I don't really know."

"I shall not speak of it," promised Colonel

57

Gresham gravely. "But how happens it that you're at the hospital? You're not sick, are you?"

"Not a bit now. I was hurt, but Dr. Dudley cured me. I'm on the staff — that's why I stay," Polly explained soberly.

"Oh! you're that little girl, are you?"

She nodded.

"I heard something about it at the time. Well, Lone Star and I will be glad to take you for a drive some other day, when you have n't any punishment on hand." He drew up the horse at the hospital entrance.

"Oh! is that his name?" exclaimed Polly. "What a loveluscious one! Would he mind if I stroked his nose?" she asked, as the Colonel lifted her down.

"He would like it very much." And they went round to the horse's head together.

"Now I must go in," Polly sighed, giving the affectionate animal a last, loving pat. "I thank you ever and ever so much, Colonel Gresham, and I should be happy to go to ride with you again some day. I hope I have n't hindered you. Good-bye."

She skipped up the long walk to the house,

the Colonel watching her until she disappeared at a side door.

Polly could not resist peeping into the Doctor's office before going upstairs. The room was empty, and she went slowly on, thinking of David.

Miss Price was standing near the door of the convalescent ward. She turned as Polly entered.

"Where have you been staying?" she asked. "Dr. Dudley came long ago."

"Yes, I know; but I was with Colonel Gresham, and I could n't get here till he did."

"Colonel Gresham! Pray, how came you with him?" Miss Price was plainly astonished.

"Why, he took me to catch the Doctor. And Lone Star got there! Oh, did n't he go! Is n't it a love — luscious name?" Polly's eyes shone.

"Child!" sighed the nurse, "what have I told you about using that word?"

"I forgot," Polly answered meekly.

"You should n't forget. I hope you did n't talk that way to Colonel Gresham."

"He would n't care," replied Polly comfortably.

"He would think you had not had proper training. Now, remember, there is no such word as loveluscious. In this case you should have said that it was a good name or a pleasing name — though it is rather too fanciful," she added.

"I love it!" cried Polly; "but it would n't sound as if I did, just to say it was good."

Then Polly's thoughts suddenly went back to Lone Star's errand.

"Oh, Miss Price!" she asked, "how is David?"

"I have not heard," was the quiet reply.

"Well, I'll go and finish up being punished now," Polly said, with a tiny sigh, and she walked over to the chair which stood where she had left it.

Miss Price did not appear to notice; but the children exchanged surprised glances. Voluntarily to continue a punishment was something with which they were unacquainted. They tried to attract Polly's attention, but her eyes were feverishly watching the half-open hall door. Dr. Dudley might stop when he came down — unless —! Her heart grew sick with the possibility.

At last she caught his step. Yes, he was coming there! Smilingly he pushed the door wide. Polly smiled in response — at least, David had not died!

"Want to come downstairs?" he invited, crossing over to her.

Still smiling, she shook her head, putting her finger to her lips.

With a puzzled look, the Doctor turned to Miss Price.

"What's happened?" he queried. "Has Polly suddenly become dumb? Or is it a game?"

"She is being punished," was the grave answer.

"Oh!" he replied. "Well, when she has been punished enough, please send her down to me."

He strode away, without one word of David, to Polly's overwhelming disappointment.

In half an hour Miss Price said, "Polly, you may go now."

She bounded off, with not even a backward glance, and the children felt lonelier

than before. But Polly's mind was too full of
David for her to think of the rest.

To her surprise the Doctor was not in his
office; but upon a book of bright color she
spied a tiny note with her name on it.
Catching it up eagerly, she read: —

DEAR THISTLEDOWN, —

Sorry to be called away, when I have invited company; but wait and take tea with
me. I shall be back soon. I've been looking
over this book, and think you will like it.

Sincerely,
ROBERT DUDLEY.

David is better.

"Oh, I'm so glad, glad, glad!" breathed
Polly, clasping the note in both her small
hands.

Then she read it once more, and afterwards established herself in the Doctor's
easiest chair, to begin the book he had suggested. If she liked the story she would tell
it to David.

Polly was so far away in thought that she
did not notice Dr. Dudley's entrance, until

he was inside the office. Then she flew to him.

He caught her in his arms, surveying her with a whimsical smile.

"All punished, are you?" he asked.

She laughed, responding with a gay affirmative.

"It does n't seem to have weighed you down much," he observed, drawing her to a seat beside him.

"It was only sitting still and not talking," she explained, "and I took two turns at it, so 't was n't bad. I told Colonel Gresham about the kerosene, and it made him laugh. Is n't Lone Star beautiful?"

"Decidedly; but how came you with the Colonel?" queried the Doctor.

"Why, he was right out there, in front of his house, and I asked him to catch you — there was n't any other way. I could n't make you hear. Oh, I do wish you could have seen Lone Star go!"

"I 'll venture he never did a more valuable service," said the Doctor fervently. "Perhaps I might add, or you either. If it had not been for your ready wits things might

63

have gone worse. I tried some new medicine for David, and it worked well, exceedingly well."

"Is he a good deal better?"

"Very comfortable. He was sleeping when I left him. Don't worry, Thistledown!" for tears stood in Polly's eyes. "I think he is going to pull through all right, and we'll have him down in the other ward before you know it."

Tea was served directly, and there were big, juicy blackberries, with which Dr. Dudley piled Polly's dish high.

When they returned to the office the story of the afternoon was finished, Polly holding back nothing, even repeating her saucy speech to the nurse.

The Doctor received it with a queer little smile.

"It was dreadfully impolite, was n't it?" she mused. "I always say impolite things when I get mad."

"Most people do," he responded. "One of the worst features of anger is that it robs us of self-control, and that is a terrible loss, if only for a moment."

64

Polly did not speak, and after a bit of a pause the Doctor went on.

"Miss Price is going through a pretty hard place just now. Word came yesterday that her only sister, who is a missionary in Turkey, is very sick and not expected to live."

"Oh, I wish I had n't said that!" Polly broke out penitently. "I might go up and tell her I'm sorry," she hesitated.

"It would n't be a bad plan," Dr. Dudley replied.

So Polly said good-night rather soberly, although carrying away with her the gay-colored book and the happy belief that David was going to get well.

Her feet lagged, as they drew near the ward. What would Miss Price say? Would she make it easy or hard for her to apologize? Then she thought of the sick sister far away in Turkey, and half forgot herself.

The nurse was writing at her little table, when she looked up to see Polly by her side.

"I'm sorry I was so saucy this afternoon," came in a soft voice. "I did n't know about your sister then. I hope she'll get well."

For a moment Miss Price did not speak,

and Polly fancied she saw tears in the black eyes.

"Thank you, my dear," she replied then. "Perhaps I was too severe. But we will be friends now, won't we?"

Polly gave a serious assent, in doubt whether she should proffer a kiss or not; but finally went away without giving the token. She had a vague feeling that Miss Hortensia Price would not care for kisses.

CHAPTER VI

ELSIE'S BIRTHDAY

FOR a week Elsie Meyer had been talking about her coming birthday, and half wishing that she could be discharged early enough to allow its celebration at home.

"Mamma always makes a cake for our birthdays," she told the children, plaintively. "Last year mine was choc'late, and year before that, jelly. Mamma said next time she'd have it orange, same's she did Ida's. Now I can't have no cake or nothin', 'count o' this old hip!" and she pouted discontentedly.

"But your arm is 'most well," suggested Polly. "That's one good thing!"

"Yes," admitted Elsie.

"And it's nice that you can be all around, instead of having to lie abed," Polly went on, hunting for happy birthday accompaniments.

"Bet you 't is!" smiled Elsie. "Lyin' abed ain't much fun, 'specially when you ache anywhere."

"If Miss Lucy was here, maybe she'd have a cake for you," put in Leonora.

"But she ain't," responded Cornelius unnecessarily.

"She ain't," echoed Otto Kriloff, his face reflecting his thought.

"When do yer s'pose she'll come back?" queried Maggie O'Donnell.

Nobody could answer.

"Maybe she never will," said Elsie gloomily, — "anyway till we all get gone."

"Oh, Elsie!" protested Polly.

"Well," was the pouting retort, "if High Price stays here much longer —"

"Sh!" hushed Cornelius, "she's comin'!" For light steps sounded along the corridor.

The children cast furtive, half-frightened glances towards the hall door; but it was not Miss Hortensia Price that smilingly opened it.

"Miss Lucy! Miss Lucy!" they shouted; and with a rush they were upon her, embracing, pulling, squeezing, until she

68

dropped into a chair, laughing and breathless.

"Have yer come to stay?" queried Maggie anxiously.

"For the present," she nodded.

A big, squealing, "O-o-h!" of joy rang through the ward, while Polly silently clung to one hand, as if she would never let it go.

"What's all this rumpus about?" came growlingly from the entrance; and the children turned, to see Dr. Dudley surveying them, his eyes a-twinkle with fun.

Polly giggled. The rest looked a bit disconcerted.

"Accept my congratulations," he said, extending his hand to the nurse.

Polly reluctantly relinquished her hold of Miss Lucy, that the physician's greeting might be properly responded to, while the young lady blushed with pleasure.

"I'm jealous," the Doctor went on, looking around on the little group. "You never make such a fuss over me when I come."

"Do yer want us to?" ventured Cornelius.

The Doctor laughed. "Well," he responded, "I'll excuse you from giving me such an ovation every day. How is that back of yours, Cornelius?" And he proceeded on his accustomed rounds.

One by one the children sidled back to Miss Lucy.

"It's my birthday to-day," announced Elsie, proceeding with her usual information regarding the home birthday cakes.

The nurse received the news with all the interest that any little girl could desire, even going so far as to "wonder" if a tea party would n't make a pleasant ending for the afternoon. That set Elsie into a flutter of blissful anticipations, so that when she overheard the Doctor telling Polly the auto would be at the door in ten minutes she forgot to wish she, too, could have a drive.

"Did you ever go to ride with Dr. Dudley?" queried Polly, as Miss Lucy buttoned her into a fresh frock.

"Oh, no!"

"Did n't he ever invite you?" she persisted.

"Of course not! Now, turn round, and let me see if you are all right."

70

"Well, he ought to! It is n't fair for me to have all the rides. He's lovely to go with!"

Miss Lucy did not answer, but her cheeks were almost as pink as Polly's dress, while she pulled out the neck ruffle and retied the ribbon that caught up the bright curls.

Polly was starting off without a word.

"Good-bye, dear! I hope you will have just as good a time as you always do." And Miss Lucy detained her long enough to leave a kiss on the red lips.

A gay little laugh was the only reply. Then Polly ran out of the dressing-room and across the ward. The children heard her tripping down the stairs, and hurried over to the windows to see her go. But nobody appeared outside, and presently Polly returned.

"Put on your hat quick, Miss Lucy!" she cried gleefully. "You're going, 'stead o' me! Dr. Dudley says he shall feel very much honored to have your company! May I get your hat?"

"Polly May!" the young woman exclaimed, in a flutter of astonishment, "what have you been telling him?"

71

"Oh, nothing much!" laughed Polly. "He wants you — so go right along!"

"Yes, do!" the children chimed in.

"Do!" echoed Elsie. "'Cause it's my birthday!"

Of course Miss Lucy insisted that she could not, would not, go. She pleaded lack of time and unsuitable dress. She summoned to her aid every excuse at command. But in the end she did exactly as the children wished, and they had the delight of seeing her drive away with the Doctor, while they chorused merry good-byes to the frantic waving of handkerchiefs.

When the automobile was out of sight, Polly thoughtfully began to paint the picture for those who had been shut off from a peep of it.

"They looked just lovely together, Miss Lucy in her pretty gray suit, with the pink rose on her hat! She waved her hand, and Dr. Dudley waved his!"

"Wonder how long they'll be gone," put in Elsie.

"I don't know — oh, say, let's clean up the dressing-room, and dust everywhere, so

72

Miss Lucy won't have it to do when she gets back!" And Polly, assured of followers, skipped away for the dust-cloths.

Of course Polly did most of the little tasks; that was to be expected, since she had no lame back or twisted leg or crutches in the way. But everybody that was on his feet had some share in the general service, and was therefore free to appropriate a part of the praise with which Miss Lucy showered them.

Yes, she had had a charming ride, she told them, and they felt it must be so, since they had never seen her in a gayer mood.

"Run up to my room if you can slip away," she whispered to Polly. "I shall be there changing my gown."

After Miss Lucy had gone, the attention of the rest was attracted by a horseback party on the street, and Polly darted away as she had been bidden.

"Dear child!" said Miss Lucy, taking the little face in both her hands. "You have given me a great pleasure."

"It was n't I," laughed Polly. "It was Dr. Dudley. Are n't you glad now that you went?"

73

"Yes," she smiled. "Because if I had n't, Elsie might not have had this birthday present. Come, see what Doctor and I bought for her."

She opened a small package, disclosing a tiny box. In the box was a little gold signet ring with an Old English "E" engraved upon it.

"Oh," admired Polly, "is n't that lovelicious! I 'm so glad for Elsie!"

"Yes," Miss Lucy went on, "I think she will like it. We wanted to give her something that she could keep to remember the day by, and we could n't think of anything better. She has a poor little home, though her mother works hard and does all she can to make the children happy. But Elsie can't have had many bright things in her life, so we 're going to try to make her birthday as pleasant as possible."

"I should think this would please anybody, it is so beautiful!" and Polly laid it gently back in its little case.

Presently she was downstairs again, happy in the knowledge of sharing a secret with Miss Lucy and Dr. Dudley.

74

After dinner she read to the children from her new book of fairy tales, and then Miss Lucy taught them some new games that they could all play — even those who were still in bed.

They were just finishing one of these, when the strains of an old song suddenly sounded near by.

"Oh, a hand-organ!" somebody shouted, and they flocked to the windows.

"And he's got a monkey!" squealed Brida.

"Oh, that's 'count o' my birthday!" cried the happy Elsie. "I do wish he'd come up here!"

Her words floated down to the organ grinder, and at once he allowed the monkey more length of cord. The little animal began to climb the wistaria vine, and presently was doffing his tiny red cap to the children, who shrieked with delight.

"Here's a penny for him, Elsie," said Dr. Dudley, who had come up behind them unnoticed.

The little birthday girl joyfully took the bright coin, and dropped it into the mon-

key's outstretched paw, receiving from him a
characteristic "thank you," which caused
more glee.

Again and again the little gay-coated messenger made trips up and down the wistaria, transferring the pennies from the children's hands to his master's pocket, until the
yellow coins finally gave out, and the Doctor
was obliged to say, "No more!"

Even then the man smilingly played on,
and when at last he and the monkey bade
their patrons good-bye, Elsie thought that
no little girl ever had so "splendid" a birthday as she was having.

The party tea was served precisely at half-
past five o'clock, and such a tea! Little
biscuits scarcely bigger than silver dollars,
small tarts filled with fig marmalade, great
berries that the children agreed were super-
bondonjical, tiny nut cookies, a frosted cake
decorated with nine pink candles, chocolate
in pretty cups, and — to top off the feast —
ice cream in the shape of chickens!

Miss Lucy and Polly and Dr. Dudley
served those little people who could not be
at the table, and nobody — not even the

birthday girl herself — enjoyed it all better than did Polly May.

Polly was eagerly anticipating the time when Elsie should be presented with the signet ring, and followed Miss Lucy's movements with watchful eyes. At last the nurse left the ward, and disappeared in the direction of her own room. The moment must be close at hand!

Dr. Dudley told funny stories, and Polly laughed with the rest; but her eyes were on the doorway, and her heart in a flutter of excitement. The moments piled up, and Miss Lucy did not come back. Polly grew anxious. Even Dr. Dudley looked at his watch, and glanced towards the door.

When, after a good quarter of an hour, the nurse returned, Polly knew that something was wrong. Dr. Dudley knew it, too; and soon he and Miss Lucy were talking together in low tones beyond the reach of Polly's ears. Had something befallen the ring? What could be the matter? The children were gleefully discussing the Doctor's last story; but Polly's thoughts were at the other end of the room. When Miss Lucy and

Dr. Dudley came back to them, however, both faces were so bright, Polly decided that she must have been mistaken, and looked for the ring to appear. But it was not so much as mentioned. The Doctor bade Elsie and the others good-bye, and Miss Lucy accompanied him into the hall.

After a while the suspense became unbearable, and Polly started for Miss Lucy's room. It was around the corner, on another corridor, and as Polly reached the turn she heard voices. Involuntarily she halted.

"It's the strangest thing," Miss Lucy was saying. "I remember laying it on the dresser after showing it to you, and then I was called away, and I can't recollect putting it in the box. I know I locked the door when I went out — I don't understand it!"

"And you say nobody but Polly has been in the room since?"

The voice belonged to Miss Curtis, one of Miss Lucy's closest friends.

"Unless it was entered with a skeleton key."

"Well, there's only one solution to the mystery, it seems to me," Miss Curtis replied.

"I won't, I won't believe it!" Miss Lucy burst out. "Polly is honesty itself. She would n't do such a thing any more than — you or I would. If it were some children — but Polly!"

"You might question her anyway; ask her if she noticed the ring when she came in after those napkins."

"I — can't! She'd see through it at once. Polly is bright. It would break her heart to know we had such a thought. I believe it got knocked off the dresser some way and will be found sooner or later; but I wanted to give it to Elsie to-day. I'm all upset about it!"

"Well, I can't help thinking —"

Polly, weak and wretched, shrank away, and went softly back through the long corridor. At the door of the ward she met Dr. Dudley.

"I was looking for you," he said. "Don't you want to take that ride you missed this morning? I have a call to go down to Linwood, and it is just cool enough now to be pleasant. Better put on your coat; your dress is thin."

79

"Could n't you — take Elsie?" faltered Polly faintly.

"Elsie? Well, Thistledown, I feel hurt! Twice in one day! Have you sworn off from auto riding?"

Usually this would have brought out a happy laugh, but now Polly merely answered, "No," very soberly.

"I should n't dare to risk a ride for Elsie until her hip is better," the Doctor resumed. "I 'll try to take her some day, when she is a little further along. Now, run and get your hat. I 'll wait for you."

Polly never quite forgot that ride. The fresh, twilight air, fragrant with dewy blossoms; the exhilarating motion; the Doctor's merry speeches; — these would have been sufficient at any other time to fill her with joy. Now she was but half conscious of them all; the dreadful ache in her heart overpowered everything else. She wondered if Dr. Dudley felt as Miss Lucy did. Or did he, with Miss Curtis, suspect her to be — a thief! She longed to cry out, "Oh, I did n't! I did n't! I did n't!" But, instead, she silently stared out on the dusky road, and wished herself at home, in her own little bed, where she could let the tears come, and not have to push them back.

She was glad, in a vague kind of way, when the auto slowed up at the hospital entrance, and the Doctor lifted her out. They walked up the flagging, hand in hand, the physician as silent as she. She would have gone directly upstairs, but he drew her into his office.

"Now, what is it, Thistledown?" he asked gently, taking her in his arms.

She hid her face on his shoulder, and began to sob.

He let the tears have their way for a time, resting his cheek lightly on her curls. Finally he spoke again.

"Is it about the ring, dear?"

She nodded.

"What have they been saying to you?" he questioned savagely.

"N-nothing to me," she replied. "I — heard — Miss Curtis — and Miss Lucy — talking. Miss Curtis — she thinks I — oh, dear! — she thinks I — took it! You don't think — I — took —"

81

"*No!*" thundered the Doctor, in so tremendous a voice that if Polly had n't been
in such depths of misery she would have
laughed outright.

As it was, she caught his hand to her lips,
and kissed it, saying, "You scared me!"

"Well, I'm sorry," he smiled; "but you
must n't ask me such questions about my
Thistledown, if you don't want to hear me
roar."

A wee giggle delighted his ears.

"Now that's something like it!" he said.
"Don't let's bother any more about that
ring. Probably we'll find it to-morrow. If
we don't, I'll buy Elsie another."

A faint, uncertain rapping made the physician set Polly gently on her feet, while he
opened the door. Nobody was in sight, and
he kept on to the main entrance.

A man stood outside, who deferentially
removed his hat.

"You b'long-a?" he asked.

"Yes, I belong here. I am Dr. Dudley.
Whom do you wish to see?"

"I play out-a here—af'-a-noon-a," with a
sweep of his hand towards the left. "Monkee

82

— him ba-ad-a monkee! Him take-a —
yours?" and he held out the missing ring.

"Oh, yes, that is ours!" the Doctor exclaimed. "We have been trying to find it. —
Polly! Polly! come here!"

Polly obeyed, though slowly, because of
her tears; but when she recognized the organ
grinder curiosity hastened her steps.

Dr. Dudley put the ring in her hand.

"Why — ee!" she cried joyously. "Elsie's ring! Oh, I'm so glad!"

"Him ba'ad-a monkee!" grinned the man.
"Him go up-a, up-a — window op'n — him
go in-a. I see nobodee — I pull-a so! Him
no come. I pull-a *so!*" and the man tugged
hard on an imaginary cord. "Him come.
Him got-a ring-a in leetle han' — I no see!
I take-a pennees — so," and he went over a
handful of invisible coins, — "I see!" pointing to the ring. "Where get-a?" He stared
wildly around, to show how great had been
his amazement. "Ah-h! — him ba-ad-a
monkee! — him get-a up-a beeg house —
beeg seeck-house — yours!" He ended with
a delighted grin, which signified his pleasure in having his surmises come true.

"We thank you very much indeed," responded Dr. Dudley earnestly, putting his hand in his pocket. "Accept this for your trouble." And he held out a quarter.

"Ah-h, no! Him ba-ad-a monkee!" He waved his hands gracefully.

He went away, however, carrying the coin, and grinning his "Good-bye."

"Was n't he funny?" laughed Polly, when the door was shut. "He called this a sick-house!"

"Why not a sick-house as well as a sick-bed?" the Doctor smiled.

But Polly only laughed, gazing down happily on the little ring.

"I'm so glad," she breathed. "Now Miss Curtis will know!"

"Miss Lucy and I knew before," was the instant reply. "Better run upstairs and let Elsie have it while it is still her birthday."

"Will you come, too?"

"No; I'll let you and Miss Lucy do the honors. There are some people I must see, and it is getting along towards sleep time. Good-night, Thistledown!" He stooped for a kiss, and she clung to him for a moment.

"It is so nice that you did n't think I did!" she whispered.

She tripped lightly upstairs, and across the ward to Miss Lucy's side. She slipped the ring into her hand.

The nurse stared her amazement.

"The monkey went in at your window, and took it!" beamed Polly. "The man's just brought it back! He never knew it till he counted his money! Oh, he told it so funny!"

"Well!" ejaculated the nurse. Then she echoed Polly's own words, "I'm so glad!"

The children were pressing near, eager to know what was exciting Miss Lucy and Polly.

"Let's see if it fits your finger, Elsie!" taking the hand of the astonished child. "Perfectly! It is a birthday present from Dr. Dudley and me. We were going to give it to you directly after tea; but when I looked for it, it was gone. Polly will tell you the rest."

And Polly did, imitating the organ grinder's words and gestures, till her listeners were shaking with laughter.

Elsie was too overpowered with joy to want to go to bed at all.

"When the lights are out I can't see my ring!" she cried in sudden dismay.

"But you can feel it," returned Polly.

"Oh! may I keep it on my finger all night long?" she asked incredulously.

"Certainly, dear," the nurse replied.

That was enough. Without another word she allowed herself to be undressed.

The ward had been dark and quiet for at least two minutes when a voice piped out, "Miss Lucy! Oh, Miss Lucy!"

"What is it, Elsie?" came the quick answer.

"I just happened to think — you and Dr. Dudley and Polly and the organ man and the monkey and everybody have been living such a splendid story for my birthday! I didn't thank you half enough!"

"You have done just right, dear. All the thanks we wanted were in your happy face. Now pleasant dreams!"

With a glad good-night, Elsie settled back contentedly on her pillow, the ring finger pressed against her cheek. And, at last, the hush of sleep brooded over the convalescent ward.

CHAPTER VII

THE LITTLE SAD LADY

DAVID grew strong steadily, but not so fast that Polly was allowed to see him as soon as they both wished. When, at last, she went up for a brief ten minutes, she was brimful of pleasure.

"I want to know about the day you ran after Dr. Dudley for me," began David, almost at once; "the time I was so sick. The Doctor said you'd tell me — he would n't, only that you had a race, and enjoyed it. I don't see how you could enjoy running your legs off for me; but it was awfully good of you."

"Why," cried Polly, "it was n't I that ran — at least, not much; it was Lone Star."

"Lone Star?" gasped David. "Polly! do tell me quick!"

"I am telling you," she laughed. "Lone Star, Colonel Gresham's beautiful horse, did the running — the trotting, I mean — why, David! what's the matter?"

The boy's eyes had grown big with excitement, and his cheeks were bright.

"Go on!" he breathed.

"That's about all. I saw I wasn't going to make the Doctor hear, and Colonel Gresham was right out there, and I told him how — sick you were, and asked him to catch the Doctor. I never thought of his taking me; but before I knew it I was in the buggy, and we were flying down the street like mad! Oh, I do wish you could have seen Lone Star go!"

"Did he know it was I?" whispered David excitedly.

"Lone Star — know?" and Polly's forehead puckered. "Oh," she brightened, "you mean the Colonel! Why, yes, of course, he did! That is, I told him — no, I didn't tell him much, though, till we were coming home. But what difference does it make?"

"Lots!" murmured David disappointedly. "I hoped he knew — oh, I hoped he knew! Polly!" — and the doll-blue eyes grew mournful — "he's my Uncle David!"

88

"Colonel Gresham — your uncle?" Now Polly's eyes widened, too.

"My mother's uncle."

"Oh, is n't that splendid!" beamed Polly. "I should think he'd have told me!"

"Probably he would n't have gone, if he'd known it was for me," went on David. "He does n't want anything to do with us. He has never forgiven mother for marrying my father; but mother loves him just the same as ever, and named me for him. I've never spoken to him, though. Queer, he should go after the Doctor for me!"

David lay quite still for a moment. When he spoke again it was on an entirely different matter, and soon the ten minutes were up.

"Did you know that David is related to Colonel Gresham?" Polly asked, as she went downstairs with Dr. Dudley.

"No; how?"

Polly told, adding what she had learned of the family history.

The Doctor shook his head sadly.

"I would n't say anything about it to the children," he cautioned her. "Such things

89

are better left untalked of. David is an unusual boy."

"When can he come down in our ward?" she questioned.

"Very soon, if he keeps on improving as fast as he has lately."

As they halted at the foot of the stairs, the Doctor looked at his watch.

"Tired?" he queried.

"Not a bit," she laughed.

"Then we'll keep on," he smiled, taking her hand again. "There is a lady I'd like you to see, one of my private patients."

"A young lady?"

"She has white hair."

"Oh, an old lady!"

"She is older than you and I."

"We are not old at all."

"And we never will grow old, will we?" twinkled the Doctor.

"We shall have to, if we live long enough."

"No, we won't; we'll always keep young."

Polly was laughing, as they entered a corridor in an "L" of the main building, a part of the hospital with which she was not familiar; but she grew grave instantly, for the

Doctor paused at a door, and she realized
that here was the lady they had come to see.

The introduction over, Polly found herself
facing a worn little woman, with weary gray
eyes, who looked more small and frail in contrast with the great oaken chair in which she
was pillowed. Mrs. Jocelyn, the Doctor had
called her, and Polly liked the sound of the
name; but she was not yet sure that she
should like the owner of it. The lady did not
smile when she said, almost as if having a
visitor bored her: —

"So you are staying here at the hospital,
Dr. Dudley tells me. What do you find to do
with yourself all day long?"

Polly had the feeling that the little sad
lady would never know whether she returned an answer or not, for her eyes seemed
to be looking at something far away. Yet
the reply was without hesitation, and primly
courteous.

"I help Miss Lucy make the beds and
dress the babies, and I dust and I carry medicine and drinks of water. Then, when there
is n't anything to do to help, I read stories
out loud, or tell them, and we play quiet

games." She paused, hunting for facts. "Oh, and I go auto riding with Dr. Dudley!" she broke out brightly. "That's very nice. And I've been to ride with Colonel Gresham!" she smiled. "I liked that, Lone Star was so splendid. Only David was awfully sick, and I was afraid he'd die, and I kept thinking of him. He said he would take me again some day."

"My dear, I don't quite understand. David Gresham sick? What David do you mean?" The little lady was waking up.

"Oh, David Collins! He's upstairs in the ward. Colonel Gresham took me to catch the Doctor."

And Polly related the story of the chase.

"Collins! Why, it was Jack Collins that Eva Gresham married — the Colonel's niece."

"Yes; David has told me that Colonel Gresham is his mother's uncle," Polly said simply.

"Well, well! So he went after the Doctor for his grand-nephew — and did n't know it till it was all over with! What strange things happen in this world! A pretty good

92

joke on David Gresham!" And the little sad lady actually smiled. Then she sighed. "It is too bad! If they'd only make up! But they never will. David isn't built on the make-up plan — or Eva either, I fancy. Eva Gresham was a beautiful girl," she rambled on, talking more to herself than to her interested listener. "She lived with her uncle from the time her parents died, when she was a tiny child. The Colonel idolized her." A bit of a break in the soft voice made a momentary pause in the musing. Then it went on again. "He had nothing in the world against Jack Collins, except that he was an artist, and poor. He would n't have been poor, they say, if he had lived. His pictures were beginning to sell at good prices."

Suddenly she came back to Polly.

"So the Colonel is going to take you driving again! Well, my dear, you need n't be afraid he'll forget it; if he said he would, he will. I declare, you look a good deal as Eva used to when she was your age. She had just such golden hair and brown eyes."

"David has blue eyes — the bluest I ever saw," observed Polly.

"He probably favors his father," replied Mrs. Jocelyn.

The Doctor's entrance put a stop to the talk, and presently Polly said good-bye, and went upstairs.

Not many days afterwards she was sent with a message to Mrs. Jocelyn's nurse, and the little lady caught sight of her at the door.

"Can't you come in and stay a while?" she called.

"I don't know," Polly hesitated, and she looked questioningly at the nurse.

"Yes, I wish you would," the young woman nodded. "I shall have to be away for a quarter of an hour or so, and if you will stay with Mrs. Jocelyn while I'm gone it will be an accommodation to me."

Polly seated herself smilingly.

"I wonder if you are as happy as you look," the little white-haired lady began.

"Oh, I'm always happy!" responded Polly; "that is, here," she added. "I could n't help being, it's so pleasant, and everybody is so good to me."

The dull gray eyes rested sadly on her. "Well, be happy while you can be," their owner said. "When you get to be old you'll forget what happiness feels like."

"Oh, but I shan't ever grow old!" laughed Polly. "Dr. Dudley and I are going to stay young!"

The little lady shook her head, and then changed the subject.

"How is David Collins getting on?"

"He is ever so much better," answered Polly; "and isn't it too bad? He's almost strong enough to come down into our ward, and there isn't any room for him! I've had to go and sleep in Miss Lucy's bed, so they could use my cot."

"Is the hospital so full as that?" scowled Mrs. Jocelyn. "Dear me, how many sick people there are!"

"There are three or four waiting now to come down, ahead of David," Polly went on. "I don't know what we shall do if he can't come at all! We've planned so many things. He said he'd tell part of the bedtime stories — oh, it was going to be lovely!"

"Perhaps there'll be a place for him pretty soon," the little lady responded. "Dr. Dudley says that you are a story-teller, too."

"Oh, yes! Some days the children keep me telling them all day long."

"Suppose you tell me one," invited the little lady.

"Well," returned Polly, a bit doubtfully, and then stopped to think over her list. "The Cherry-Pudding Story," which usually insisted on being uppermost, would scarcely do this time, she thought. It seemed too rollicking for this big, hushed room, with only one sober-eyed listener. She hastily decided that none of the cat stories were suitable, or fairy tales — "Oh!" she suddenly dimpled, "I wonder if you would n't like the story that David lent me. His aunt wrote it, and sent it to him. I read it to Miss Lucy and the children. It is about little Prince Benito and a wonderful flower."

"I shall be pleased to hear it," was the polite reply.

This seemed somewhat doubtful to Polly, used as she was to enthusiastic responses.

"Won't it tire you?" she hesitated.

"I am always tired, little one. Perhaps the story will rest me."

"Then I'll run right upstairs and get it,"

beamed Polly. "I guess I can read it better than I can tell it. You don't mind staying alone while I'm gone?"

"No, indeed!" was the reply, yet she sighed after Polly had disappeared. All the brightness of the room seemed to have vanished.

The little sad woman soon found herself watching for the light returning footfalls, and she greeted the child with a faint smile.

Polly read as she talked, naturally and with ease, and before she had finished the first page of the story her listener had settled herself comfortably among her pillows, a look of interest on her usually spiritless face.

It was a fanciful tale of a beautiful little prince who, by sowing seeds of the Wonderful White Flower of Love, transformed his father's kingdom, a country desolate from war and threatened by famine and insurrection, into a land of prosperity and peace and joy.

At the last word, Polly, flushed with the spirit of the story, looked up expectantly; but her listener's weary eyes seemed to be studying the pattern of the dainty comfort across her lap. Sadly Polly gathered together the scattered manuscript sheets, and waited.

"Thank you, dear," the little lady finally said; but the words were spoken as with an effort.

"I am afraid I have tired you," mourned Polly.

"No, little one; you have only given me something to think of. You read unusually well. Perhaps we'll have another story some day. You don't need to stay, if you have anything else to do. I shall want nothing until Miss Parkin comes."

Polly felt that she was dismissed, yet she had promised the nurse to remain. She hesitated a moment, and then said, "Good-bye," and went out. She met Miss Parkin in the hall, and explained.

Up in the ward, Miss Lucy was quick to see that Polly was troubled.

"How did the story go?" she asked.

"I don't know," Polly sighed. "I guess she did n't like it, 'cause she seemed to be thinking about something else, and she said I need n't stay any longer. I thought it

98

would make her happier," she lamented, "and all it did was to tire her!" Polly's eyes were brimming over with tears.

"Never mind, dear," said Miss Lucy comfortingly. "You did your part, and as well as you could; that's all any of us can do. So don't worry about it. There's Brida looking this way, as if she were just longing to talk with you."

"She shan't wait another minute," smiled Polly, and off she skipped, to make Brida and her followers merry.

CHAPTER VIII

A WARNING FROM AUNT JANE

TOWARDS noon came a telephone call for Polly to go down to Dr. Dudley's office. Usually she sped gladly to obey such a summons; now she was assailed by a sudden fear.

"Have I made her very much worse?" was her instant inquiry, as the Doctor opened his door.

"Made whom worse?" he questioned.

"Why, Mrs. Jocelyn!"

"I have heard nothing from her. What is it?"

Polly told of her visit and of the reading.

"Is that all!" the Doctor laughed. "Don't worry about it any more, little girl! Your stories are not the kind that harm people. What did you read? One that I know?"

"I don't think so," Polly replied. "I did n't tell you about Prince Benito, did I?"

The physician shook his head. "Suppose you tell it to me now," he suggested.

So, perched comfortably upon the arm of his chair, Polly related the story of "The Wonderful White Flower."

"I see," he mused, as Polly stopped speaking. He was silent a moment. Then he went on.

"Mrs. Jocelyn lost her only child, a beautiful little boy, when he was eight years old. It is not unlikely that this story awakened tender memories."

"I'm sorry I made her feel bad," grieved Polly.

"I wouldn't be if I were you."

A "Why!" of wonder was rounding Polly's lips, as the physician continued: —

"Perhaps you have done Mrs. Jocelyn more good than you will ever know. Since her husband and little boy died she has shut people out of her life, seldom leaving her home, and rarely entertaining a guest. From what she has said to me I judge that she has allowed herself to brood over her sorrows till she has become bitter and melancholy. Let's hope that your little story will open her eyes."

"Does she live all alone when she is home?" queried Polly.

"Alone with her servants."

"Oh, then she is n't poor! I thought she must be."

Dr. Dudley smilingly shook his head. "She has more money than probably you or I will ever handle, little girl; but we'll have better riches than gold, won't we?"

"Yes; you'll make people well, and I'll try to make them happy," returned Polly, a sweet seriousness on her usually merry face. "I wish I could make everybody in the world happy," she added.

"That is too big a job for one little Thistledown," laughed Dr. Dudley. "There!" he exclaimed, "I nearly forgot what I called you down for! Colonel Gresham hailed me out here, and asked if you could go to Forest Park, this afternoon, with him and Lone Star. I said yes. Was that all right?"

"Of course!" beamed Polly. "Is n't it lovely of him to ask me? Had I better tell him that David is better?"

"Not unless he inquires," the Doctor answered. "He said he would be here at three o'clock. You can come down a little before that, and keep a lookout for him, so as not to make him wait."

Polly was on hand, in the Doctor's office, while it still lacked fifteen minutes of the hour; but the Colonel was early, and the waiting time was short. Very sweet she looked, as she ran down the stone walk to the street, in her dainty new white dress with simple ruffles edging neck and sleeves. In the delight of the moment Polly did not forget the children up at the ward windows, but waved them a gay good-bye, while Colonel Gresham greeted the bobbing heads with a graceful swing of his straw hat.

There was not much talk at first, for the way to the park lay through the heart of the city; but Polly was content silently to watch the changing throngs around them.

Suddenly the Colonel drew up his horse in response to a call from the sidewalk, and presently was in a business talk with the man who had arrested him.

"I shall have to leave you for a moment," he said, at length, turning to Polly. "I'll be back shortly." And, having fast-

103

ened Lone Star, he disappeared up a stair-
way.

Polly was enjoying this little break,when
she caught sight of a well-known face. "It's
Aunt Jane!" she murmured, and was
promptly seized with a desire to hide.
Breathlessly she watched the woman in the
black dress, hoping for escape from those
ferret eyes; but the horse and carriage were
conspicuous, and Aunt Jane's glance fell first
on Lone Star and then passed to the little
girl upon the seat.

"Polly May!" she exclaimed, and Polly
smiled a somewhat uncertain greeting.

"How in the world did you come here?"
twanged the remembered voice.

"Colonel Gresham is taking me to ride,"
was the explanation, "and he's gone upstairs a minute."

"Colonel Gresham! Goodness gracious
me! Well, you are comin' up in the world!
Why hain't you been round to see me?"

"I'm — pretty busy," answered Polly,
"I —"

"Busy! Huh, you must be! Well, so 'm I
busy, or I should 'a' been up after you before

this. Guess you've stayed at that hospital 'bout long enough. You might 's well be helpin' me as gallivantin' round with Tom, Dick, and Harry."

"I — thought I was going to stay all summer," faltered Polly.

"I did n't make no special agreement, and now there's cannin' and picklin' and whatnot to do, I could keep you out o' mischief easy. Where'd you get that dress?"

"Miss Lucy bought it for me."

"She did, hey? Well, 't ain't hurt with trimmin', is it?"

The Colonel appearing at the moment, Aunt Jane made a rather hurried departure, while she assured Polly that she would "be round before long."

"Who is that woman?" inquired Colonel Gresham.

"My Aunt Jane," was the soft answer.

"What's her other name?"

"Mrs. Simpson. Uncle Gregory — that was her husband — was killed when the building fell, and I was hurt."

"Oh, yes! I recollect. Well, is Aunt Jane good to you? Do you love her very much?"

105

Polly waived the first question, and proceeded to the second. "I'm afraid I don't love her at all," she replied honestly. "Of course, I ought to; but I don't."

"It is mighty hard to love some folks," meditated the Colonel. "I think I should rather do a season's ploughing than to attempt to love that Aunt Jane."

Polly smiled, and then returned to the question she had left behind. "I guess she's pretty good to me," she said. "She never whipped me."

"Whipped you!" the Colonel exclaimed. "I should hope not!"

"Aunts do whip sometimes," Polly nodded soberly. "Bessie Jackson's aunt whipped her — awful! I'd run away!"

"Yes," the Colonel agreed, "that would be the best thing in such a case — though perhaps this Bessie deserved the whipping."

"No, she did n't!" Polly assured him.

"Well, now, I'll tell you," he went on confidentially, "if anybody ever lays a finger on you, just you come to my house, and I'll see that you are treated all right. Remember that now!"

Polly chuckled a "thank you," and Colonel Gresham began talking about the park, the entrance of which they were nearing.

Polly tried to put Aunt Jane from her mind; but the threatened possibilities kept thrusting themselves into the Colonel's merry speeches, until she scarcely comprehended what he was saying. Little by little, however, the beauties of her surroundings overpowered all else, and Aunt Jane was for the time almost forgotten.

The wise men who had planned Forest Park had known better than to try to improve on nature's handiwork, and rocks and ravines, brooks and pools, wooded slopes and ferny tangles, were left practically unchanged. Polly loved birds and flowers and all the scents and sounds of summer fields and woods, and now, as the air came laden with faint perfume, and a carol burst into the stillness, she clasped her little hands together with a soft breath of delight.

Colonel Gresham watched her in furtive silence. Finally she turned towards him.

"I should think it would make sick people well to come out here, should n't you?"

"Some of them," he nodded.

"I'm going to tell Mrs. Jocelyn all about it. Perhaps it would make her happier if she'd come."

"What Mrs. Jocelyn is that?" asked the Colonel.

"I don't know her other name. The one that's at the hospital — she's small, and has white hair. Her husband and little boy died."

"Oh, yes! Juliet Jocelyn, probably; but I didn't know that she was sick."

"She's had an operation, I think; but she's getting well now. I've been to see her twice. Yesterday I read her a story."

"I hope she appreciated it," observed the Colonel dryly.

"I'm not sure," Polly replied; "she didn't say. Do you know Mrs. Jocelyn?"

"I knew her a long time ago," was the grave answer, as he turned his horse into the road that wound up the eastern side of the mountain.

"Oh, you're going to take the Cliff Drive!" cried Polly delightedly. "Dr. Dudley couldn't go, because they won't let autos up there."

108

"No, for one might meet a skittish horse. I like to come up here once in a while for the view."

"I'm not going to look till we get clear up," Polly declared. And resolutely she kept her eyes the other way.

"Now!" announced Colonel Gresham.

Polly turned her head — and held her breath. Then she let it out in one long sigh of rapture.

Before them lay the city, glittering in the afternoon sunshine, while beyond, to the north and east and south, green hills formed a living frame for the picture.

"It is worth coming for," said the Colonel, at last. "There is your home — see?"

"Oh, yes! It looks like a castle in a forest."

And then — when joy was uppermost — Aunt Jane's threat crowded in.

Polly's eyes wandered from the "castle" in the direction of the home she dreaded.

Colonel Gresham noted the sudden shadow on the bright face, and took up the reins.

On the way back they stopped at a confectioner's, and the Colonel brought out a package and laid it on Polly's lap. "There is something to remember the drive by," he said.

"Oh, thank you!" she beamed. "But I don't need anything more to make me remember it," she added. "It has been beautiful — right straight through ! — Except Aunt Jane!" she put in honestly, under her breath, and again her face was shadowed.

"It is the best way," observed the Colonel, "to let disagreeable things slip off our shoulders at once. If we should carry them all, we should have a sorry load."

"I guess I'll do that way," smiled Polly; "but Aunt Jane don't slip easy!"

"Shake her off," laughed the Colonel, "and she'll go!"

It was a happy moment up in the ward when Polly opened her box of candy. Such chocolates, such candied cherries and strawberries, with tiny tongs to lift them with, the children had never seen. They chose one apiece all round, which Miss Lucy said was enough for that day, and Polly carried the box down to the Doctor's office, that he might taste her sweets. It never occurred to

110

her that she was entitled to more than the others.

Dr. Dudley heard all about the drive, but nothing of Aunt Jane. Polly had decided to take the Colonel's advice — if she could, and she recollected with relief that Aunt Jane was always more ready to threaten than to perform.

A few days afterwards Dr. Dudley sent early for Polly.

"Anyway it is n't Aunt Jane at this time," she assured herself, as she ran downstairs.

"Mrs. Jocelyn wants to see you right away," the Doctor told her.

"She does?" wondered Polly. "Do you know for what?"

"I don't *know* anything," he smiled; "but I *guess* a good deal."

"Oh! what do you guess it is?" she entreated.

He shook his head laughingly. "I should hate to have you discover that I was n't a good guesser," he said. "Run along, and find out for sure!"

Polly was astonished to see how greatly the

111

little lady had changed. Her cheeks reflected the delicate pink of the robe she was wearing, and her eyes were glad. Her voice was full of eagerness.

"Here comes the little sunbeam!" she smiled. "Did I interrupt any task or play?" She drew Polly within the circle of her arm. "I could n't wait another moment to thank you for reading me that story of the little prince. It brought back my own little Lloyd, who was always planting those seeds of love wherever he went. But since he left me I have been like that forgetful queen mother, too wrapped up in myself to think of others. Now I am going to begin to grow those 'wonderful white flowers.'" Her eyes shone through tears.

Polly did not know what to say; she only looked her sympathy and appreciation.

"Tell me about David," the little lady went on. "Is he well enough to come downstairs?"

"Yes, he's all ready," was the reply; "but he's got to wait for somebody to go. Elsie was to leave to-day or to-morrow; but she needs a little more treatment, Dr. Dudley

says. So I don't know when David can
come."

"I know!" responded Mrs. Jocelyn confi-
dently. "He is coming down to the convalescent ward — let me see, I think it may
be this afternoon, but to-morrow morning
sure!"

"Wh-y! how can he?" gasped Polly.
"There are three ahead of him, and there
are n't any more beds!"

"There will be before long," chuckled the
little lady gayly. "I have been having a bit
of a talk with Dr. Dudley, and he tells me
that there is plenty of room in your ward for
six or more cots — and Polly May is going to
buy them! That is, she can if she chooses."

Polly's face was one big interrogation
point. "Why! I don't —" she began, but
was interrupted by a kiss right on her lips.

"Oh, you dear, precious little innocent!"
cried Mrs. Jocelyn. "Read that, and see if it
will tell you anything!" She took a strip of
paper from the table, and put it into Polly's
hand.

Across the top, in large letters, was the
name of a bank. The rest was partly printed

and partly written. Polly read wonderingly:—

Pay to the order of Polly May Three Hundred Dollars.

JULIET P. JOCELYN.

"O-o-h!" and Polly's face was beautiful in its joy; "does this mean that you're going to give me three hundred dollars to buy some new cots with?"

"It means that the money is your own to use exactly as you please." The little lady was scarcely less excited than the child. Giving was to her almost an untried pleasure.

"Oh, I can't, I can't, I can't thank you enough! It is so lovelicious!" Then Polly threw her arms around the happy donor in a way that would have made her cry out with actual pain if she had not been too delighted to realize it.

"I think that will cover the cost of six or seven cots, equipped for use," said Mrs. Jocelyn, — "that is, if you wish to spend the money for them." The gray eyes actually twinkled.

114

"Why, of course I do!" cried Polly. "What else could I do with it?"

"*You* couldn't, you blessed child! So we'll have David downstairs just as soon as his bed is ready, won't we?"

"Yes, and how glad he'll be! Oh, how glad he'll be! And Brida and Elsie — they've been dreadfully afraid they'd have to go home before he came down; they want to see him so! Won't they be pleased!"

"I want to see David, too," declared the little lady, "and he must come down with you as soon as he is strong enough — unless I get well first," she laughed. "I feel almost well now."

Polly beamed her delight, and presently was racing upstairs to tell her good news to everybody.

Dr. Dudley managed to get away before noon for the pleasant errand of purchasing the beds, and Polly was overflowing with bliss. She had her choice in everything, with the Doctor and the merchant as advisers; and although the bill footed up to a little more than the check, the difference was struck off, and the cots and bedding pro-

mised to be at the hospital by two o'clock
that afternoon.

The convalescent ward was in such an
ecstasy of excitement that dinner went
poorly; but finally it was cleared away, and
the cots moved to make room for those that
were coming. Everybody helped that could
walk — even those that had to hobble on
crutches, for there were many little things to
do, and only a short time to do them in.
Polly was Miss Lucy's ready right hand,
with always a flock of eager assistants. When
the beds were actually in place, and the men
had gone away, came the delightful task
of spreading on the sheets and blankets and
pretty coverlets. All was in readiness before the hour specified, and then there was
nothing to do but to wait for the coming of
the new patients.

At last there were footsteps on the stairs,
uneven footsteps, as of one bearing a burden
— the children had started! David was the
last, and Polly had begun to be troubled,
lest, after all, something might have delayed
him until another day. But there he was,
smiling to her, and waving a thin little hand

in greeting. Polly wished that Mrs. Jocelyn could be there to see it all. When David was finally in bed, with Polly by his side, he said: —

"Now, tell me all about it, please! It was such a splendid surprise!"

So Polly told just how it had happened, and talked and kept on talking, until she suddenly discovered that David was looking a little weary — though he insisted that he was not tired. But in her motherly way, that was the delight of the ward, she bade him shut his eyes and "go right to sleep," giving his hand a final caressing pat, and then running away to let him have a chance to follow her injunction.

CHAPTER IX

A NIGHT OF SONG

DAVID had been nearly three whole days in the convalescent ward, taking big leaps on the road to health, when Polly was summoned to Dr. Dudley's office. Since her meeting with Aunt Jane, the sharp-voiced woman was ever close at hand, ready instantly to appear in the little girl's thought and fill her with sickening fear. Now Polly's feet lagged as she went downstairs; she dreaded to look into the office. But Dr. Dudley was there quite alone, smiling a blithe good-morning.

"Miss Price wishes your assistance in the care of a patient," he began.

"Wh-y!" breathed Polly, "how funny — for her to want me!"

"She is nursing Burton Leonard," the physician explained, "a little six-year-old boy who was operated upon yesterday for appendicitis. His life depends on his being quiet, but he will not keep still. Miss Price thinks you can help out by telling him a story or two, something that will make him forget, if possible, how terribly thirsty he is."

"Can't he have anything to drink?" questioned Polly, with a sympathetic little frown.

"Only an occasional sip of warm water — nothing cold."

"I'll do my best," she promised. "I shall love to help, if I can."

Dr. Dudley took her hand, and down the corridor they went, the one with long strides, the other on dancing feet.

Master Burton stared at his visitor, his big black eyes looking bigger in contrast with the white, drawn little face.

"What you come for?" he asked fretfully.

"To see you," smiled Polly.

"I do' want to be seen," was the unexpected reply, and he pulled the sheet over his head.

Polly laughed, and waited.

Presently the black eyes again appeared.

"Why don't you lie abed?" he whined.

119

"I did till I got well."

"Did they make you lie still?" he questioned.

"Yes, I had to keep very still indeed."

"I don't," he whispered, glancing towards the Doctor, who was just passing out. "When they ain't lookin' I wriggle round!"

"You'd get well quicker if you'd do just as Miss Price and Dr. Dudley tell you," advised Polly.

"Huh! my mamma says nobody on earth can make me mind!" He beckoned her nearer. "Say," he chuckled, "she put an ice bag on me," with a wink towards the nurse, *"and I got out some o' the ice!* It's awful good! She would n't give me a drop o' water, only horrid old warm stuff." He showed his tongue, with a bit of ice upon it.

Polly was shocked. In the light of what the physician had told her, she realized that the boy was ignorantly thwarting the efforts of those who were trying to save his life. She did not know what to say.

"Do you like stories?" she finally asked.

The lad looked surprised, but answered, "Some kinds. Why?"

"I thought I'd tell you one, if you'd like me to."

"Do you know one 'bout soldiers?"

"I don't believe I do; but I know a song about a soldier."

"Can you sing?"

"Yes."

"Sing, then."

"Will you lie still if I will?" asked Polly.

"It's a go!"

So Polly sang the old, old song of "The Drummer Boy of Waterloo," one that her grandmother had taught her when she was a wee girl.

The boy was true to his promise, and remained motionless until the last note ceased.

"Sing it again!" he commanded. "That's a dandy!"

Twice, three times more, the sad little ditty was sung; then the sweet voice slipped softly into Holland's "Lullaby," which had been learned from hearing it sung by Miss Lucy to restless little patients.

"Rockaby, lullaby, bees in the clover,
    Crooning so drowsily, crying so low.
Rockaby, lullaby, dear little rover,

121

> Down into wonderland,
> Down to the underland,
> Down into wonderland go!
>
> . . . .
>
> "Rockaby, lullaby, dew on the clover!
>   Dew on the eyes that will sparkle at dawn.
> Rockaby, lullaby, dear little rover,
>   Into the stilly world,
>   Into the lily world,
>   Into the lily world gone!"

Before Polly reached the last word the song had died almost to a breath, for Burton was "gone" — fast asleep. For a time she watched him. His breathing was slow and steady. Finally she slipped softly from her chair, and glanced across the room. Miss Price nodded and smiled, and Polly tip-toed towards the door, beckoning her to follow.

Outside, in the corridor, the nurse heard of the mischievous act of her little patient.

"I did n't think he would do that!" sighed Miss Price, and she shook her head gravely. "You are right to tell me at once," she went on; "but I will not let Burton know that I learned of it through you. Thank you for coming down. You may like to hear," she added, as Polly was starting away, "that I had good news from Turkey this morning. My sister is better; they think she is going to get well."

"Oh, I'm so glad!" beamed Polly. Then, impulsively, she put up her arms, and the next minute they were around the neck of Miss Hortensia Price.

This time she felt sure that the stately nurse did like kisses, else why should she return them so cordially, and presently Polly was skipping upstairs, full of gladness that her service had been a success.

That night, in the hour before bedtime, David was entertainer. Polly had promised the children delightful stories from him, and now he made good her word. He chose for his recital something of his aunt's that Polly had never heard, the true account of how some little tricksy Southern boys obtained a pet goat. David had shown his wisdom in making his first selection a story that would please the crowd. The children laughed and laughed over it, and begged for another. The second was as unlike the first as possible. It was about a little princess who was carried

123

into captivity by some rough people, and who won the hearts of everybody, even those of her captors, by her gentleness and love, and who finally, through her brave unselfishness, found her way to freedom and happiness.

"I 'd love to be like that Princess Yvonne," sighed Polly.

It was in David's heart to say, "You are more nearly like her than any girl I ever saw," but the words were not spoken. He only smiled across to Miss Lucy, who sent him a smile of comprehension in return. These two had quickly learned to understand each other without words.

"It is so hard always to love everybody," Polly went on. She was thinking of Aunt Jane. "Do you love everybody, Miss Lucy, — every single body?"

The nurse laughed softly. "I'm afraid I sometimes find it a difficult task," she admitted; "but even when we dislike people, or do not exactly love them, we can wish them well, and be ready to do them kindnesses whenever it is possible. And we can usually find something lovable in everybody,

if we look for it deep enough and long
enough."

There was a moment's hush, and then Elsie
piped out: —

"David, can't you tell another story,
please?"

"It is pretty nearly bedtime," Miss Lucy
suggested. "If we have one, it must be
short."

"Oh, David, sing a song — do!" begged
Polly.

"Can he sing?" queried Cornelius wonderingly.

"Beautifully!" answered Polly.

"You don't know!" laughed David.
"You never heard me."

"Yes, I do know!" insisted Polly. "They
would n't let you sing solos at St. Paul's
Church if you did n't sing well — so!"

The children waited in astonished silence.
This was an accomplishment of David's
which had not been told them.

Miss Lucy propped him up a little higher
among his pillows, and then he began the
sweet vesper hymn, "The King of Love my
Shepherd is."

The children were very quiet until they were sure that the singing was over. Then Brida voiced everybody's thought.

"Was n't that beautiful!"

Presently Polly was going about her little nightly tasks humming the melody to herself. She was quick to catch an air, and with a bit of prompting from David she soon had the words.

"Oh, you and David can sing it to us together to-morrow night!" cried Elsie, and there was a responsive chorus from all over the ward.

Polly went to sleep singing the hymn in her heart.

Miss Lucy's cot was nearest the door, and shortly after midnight she waked with the sound of a rap in her ears. Hastily throwing on a robe which was always at hand, she answered with a soft, "What is it?"

"Burton Leonard is worse," came in Dr. Dudley's low voice, "and he wants Polly to sing to him. Get her ready as quick as you can, please."

The little girl was dreaming of Aunt Jane. She was trying to hold a tall ladder straight up in the air, while Aunt Jane climbed to the top, and her aunt was fretting because she did not keep it steady. "Oh, I can't hold on a minute longer!" Polly dreamed she was saying to herself. "But I must! I must! because Miss Lucy said we were to do kindnesses for anybody we did n't love!"

Then she roused enough to know that Miss Lucy was bending over her, whispering:

"Polly dear! can you wake up?"

"Oh! David?" Polly's first thought was for her friend.

"No, darling; David's all right. Dr. Dudley wants you to come down and sing to little Burton Leonard."

"Oh, of course I'll go!" Polly was wide awake now, and ready for anything.

She and Miss Lucy made speedy work of the dressing. Dr. Dudley was outside the door waiting for her, and quietly they went downstairs.

"I'll have to sing pretty soft; shan't I?" she questioned; "or it will disturb other folks."

"Yes," the physician agreed. "But the room is rather isolated anyway, at the end of the wing. There 's nobody near that there 's any danger of harming."

"Hullo!" came in a weak little voice, as Polly entered the doorway. "I told 'em I'd keep still if you'd sing to me; but I did n't b'lieve you'd come. I thought you'd be too sleepy."

The boy's mother was nervously smoothing his pillow, but at a word from the physician she retired to a seat beside the nurse.

A small electric light glowed at the other end of the apartment, and the night wind blew in at the open window, fluttering the leaves of a magazine that lay near. Polly felt awed by the hush of seriousness that seemed to fill the room. Although the Doctor spoke in his usual tone, the voices of the others scarcely rose above a whisper. She was glad when Dr. Dudley took her upon his knee. His encircling arm gave her instant cheer.

"Sing 'bout the 'Drummer Boy'!" begged the sick child, plaintively, and there was something in his tone that gave Polly a pang of fear. How different from his commands of the morning!

128

Very soft was the singing, as if in keeping with the occasion and the hour, yet every word was clear.

From "The Drummer Boy" Polly slipped easily into "The Star-Spangled Banner," "America," "Columbia, the Gem of the Ocean," and "The Battle Hymn of the Republic." Then came two or three negro melodies and some songs she had learned at school, at the end of which Dr. Dudley whispered to her to stop and rest.

While she was singing, the sick boy had lain motionless; but now he began to nestle, and called fretfully, "Water! water! do give me some water!"

The nurse fetched a glass, but as soon as he discovered that it was warm, he would not taste it.

"Sing more!" he pleaded.

So again Polly sang, beginning with "My Old Kentucky Home," and then charming the Doctor with one of his favorites, "'Way down upon the Swanee Ribber." "Annie Laurie" came next, then "Those Evening Bells," and other old songs which her grandmother had taught her.

129

"I'm afraid you're getting too tired," Dr. Dudley told her; but she smilingly shook her head, and sang on.

Once or twice the lad drowsed, and she stopped for a bit of a rest, until his insistent, "Sing more!" roused her from a momentary dream.

The mother sat a little apart, but kept her eyes on her boy's face, ready for instant service.

Several times the physician reached over to feel his patient's pulse, and seemed satisfied with what he found.

So the night dragged by.

It was early dawn when Miss Price, in answer to the repeated call, again fetched water, and, as before, the child refused it.

"Take away that nasty old hot stuff, and bring me some cold!" he commanded, with a spurt of his usual lordliness.

The nurse gently urged him to taste it; but he only pushed the spoon away.

Dr. Dudley was about to speak, when Polly interposed with the first lines of "The Secret," a little song she had learned in her last days of school. Her voice was loud enough to catch the boy's attention, but the words were sung slowly and confidentially.

> "What do you think is in our back yard?
> P'rhaps you can guess, if you try real hard.
> It is n't a puppy, or little white mice,
> But it's something that's every bit as nice!
> Oh, no, it's not chickens or kittens at all!"

She broke off, her eyes smilingly meeting Burton's.

"What is it?" he asked feebly.

"Take some of that," she replied, pointing to the cup, and I'll sing "the rest."

He frowned at her, as she leaned back on the Doctor's shoulder. In her attitude he saw nothing of hope, unless he complied with her requirement. Without another protest he swallowed a few spoonfuls of the liquid.

Then Polly went on.

> "Can't you think what is soft and round and small?
> It's two little — somethings, as white as snow!
> *Two dear baby rabbits!* — there, now — you know!"

"Sing it again!" he begged.

Soon his eyelids dropped together, but as the song was ended he opened them wide, with a silent appeal for more.

So the tired little girl sang the lullaby that

had put him to sleep early the day before. This time it did not have the hoped-for effect, and the vesper hymn which David had sung — at the bedtime hour which now seemed so very far away — came to the singer's mind. Softly she began the tender little song, going through it without a break.

At its close the boy lay quite still, and with a sigh of relief her bright head drooped on the pillowing shoulder.

The Doctor leaned forward, and listened. The lad's breathing was soft and regular.

"Sound asleep at last! Now, Thistledown — a-h!" he gasped, for Polly lay on his arm, a limp little heap.

With great strides he carried her to the window.

The nurse reached the couch as soon as he, and thrust a globule into his hand.

Crushing it in his handkerchief, he passed it before the child's nostrils, and with a little fluttering breath the brown eyes opened.

"I guess — I — was — a little tired," Polly said brokenly.

"You were faint — that's all. Don't try to talk."

132

Miss Price brought some medicine in a glass, and Polly obediently swallowed the draught.

"Is she all right now?" whispered Mrs. Leonard, who had been standing back, frantically clasping and unclasping her nervous little hands.

The nurse nodded. "For a minute I was afraid — she is not very strong; but it was only a faint."

"If anything had happened, I should never have forgiven myself for letting her sing so long! But did n't he go off to sleep beautifully. Just look at him — still as a mouse!" And the two moved nearer the bed.

Polly went upstairs in Dr. Dudley's arms.

"I can — walk," she murmured.

"No; I want the pleasure of carrying you," was the light response, and for answer a soft little hand stroked his own.

Miss Lucy met them at the door of the ward, and her face was white with fear.

"She was tired and a little faint," the Doctor explained. "I thought I'd better bring her up."

"Don't worry — Miss Lucy!" smiled

Polly. "I'm — all right." She sighed softly, as her head touched the pillow.

"Precious child!" murmured the nurse, and then followed the Doctor to the door.

"Has she been singing all this time?" Reproach was in the gentle tone.

He bowed. "I know! It was too severe a strain. But she did n't seem very tired until just at the last — and it has probably saved the boy's life."

"That is good — if it has n't hurt her," Miss Lucy added anxiously.

"I think not," he replied. "She seems to be all right now. She will probably sleep late from exhaustion. Do you suppose you can keep the children quiet?"

"Quiet? Bless them! they won't stir, if they know it is going to disturb Polly!"

Dr. Dudley laughed softly. "Don't let her get up till I come," he charged her. "I'll be in early." And he turned away.

Miss Lucy undressed Polly so gently that she did not awake. Then she sat by her side until broad daylight. The children were still asleep around her, when her name was whispered across the ward.

David was sitting up in bed, his face shadowed with fear.

"What's the matter with Polly?" he questioned.

Miss Lucy told briefly the incident of the night, and he lay down again, but not to sleep. If the nurse so much as stirred, David was always looking her way.

The ward was greatly excited at the news; but Miss Lucy had been true in her predictions. Never had such noiseless toilets been made within its walls. Everybody went about on tiptoe, and Leonora Hewitt would not walk at all, lest the thump of her crutch on the floor might waken Polly.

The little girl was still asleep when Dr. Dudley came, but soon afterward she opened her eyes to find him at her side. Almost her first words were an inquiry about Burton Leonard.

"He is very much better," the Doctor replied. "He wanted me to tell you not to worry about him to-day, for he would keep still without your singing. I did n't know there was such good stuff in him. He has been angelic, Miss Price says, ever since he

135

heard that you were tired out. That seemed
to touch his little heart. He calls you 'a
dandy girl.' You have quite won him over."

"I'm glad," smiled Polly. "I guess I can
sing a little for him to-day, if he needs me."

"You won't!" Dr. Dudley replied. "You
are to stay in bed, Miss Polly May! When
young ladies are out all night they must lie
abed the next day."

"All day long?" she queried.

"Yes."

Polly sighed a bit of a sigh; then she
smiled again.

"I may talk, may n't I?" she begged.

"Not many bedside receptions to-day," he
answered. "I want you to sleep all you can."

With a little chuckle she shut her eyes
tight. "Good-night!" she said demurely.

"That is a gentle hint for me to go," the
Doctor laughed. Then he bent for a whisper
in her ear. "If you sleep enough to-day, I
think we 'll have a ride to-morrow."

She opened her eyes, returned a happy
"thank you," and then cuddled down on her
pillow.

CHAPTER X

THE WARD'S ANNIVERSARY

THE convalescent ward was generally a happy place, for everybody was getting well, and getting well is pleasant business. Just now it was at its best. The majority of the children had lived together long enough to be loyal friends, and there were no discordant dispositions. In fact, discords knew better than to push in where Miss Lucy reigned. Her gentle tact had proved quite sufficient for any disagreeable element that had yet appeared in the ward, and lately all had been harmony. The nurse would have told you that this was greatly due to Polly May, and Polly would have insisted that it was entirely Miss Lucy's work; but as long as happiness was there nobody cared whence it came.

David Collins was a decided acquisition; the ward agreed in that.

"He can tell stories almost as well as

137

Polly," declared Elsie Meyer to a knot of her chosen intimates.

"Not qui-te," objected loyal little Brida, glancing over her shoulder to make sure that they were far enough away from the ears of the boy under discussion.

"I did n't say quite," returned Elsie, in a lower voice, "I said almost. 'Course, nobody tells 'em so good as Polly — she's 'special!"

"But David is a dandy fine feller!" asserted Cornelius. "He can play ball, reg'lar baseball! A college feller on a team showed him how!"

"Wisht I could play ball," sighed Leonora Hewitt, a bit dejectedly.

"Girls don't play baseball!" laughed Cornelius.

"They do some kinds anyway—I used to!" And again Leonora sighed. It is hard to be shut out from things when you are only ten.

"I would n't care, if I were you," comforted Elsie, in a way that showed her to be an unconscious pupil of her adored Polly. She threw an arm around the little girl who

138

the Doctor feared would never walk again on two strong feet. "There's lots of things better than playing ball."

"What?" demanded Cornelius, with more curiosity than thoughtfulness.

Elsie flashed him a look that meant, "How can you?" for Cornelius had been able to throw aside his own helps to walking. Then she answered triumphantly, "Playing with dolls — for one thing!"

"Dolls!" echoed Cornelius, laughing. "Ho, ho! dolls!"

"Well, I don't care, they are! Ain't they, Miss Lucy?"

"What is it, Elsie?" smiled the nurse across from her desk. "I was n't noticing."

"Dolls — ain't dolls more fun than playing ball?"

"That depends," answered Miss Lucy. "Cornelius or Moses would no doubt enjoy a game of ball better than the prettiest doll that ever was made; but you and Leonora and Corinne, for instance, would be unusual little girls if you did n't like dolls best."

Elsie and Cornelius faced each other with good-natured laughter.

"But I hain't got any doll," lamented Leonora.

"Nary a ball!" declared Cornelius, striking his breast dramatically. "So we're even!"

"My doll's 'most worn out," mourned Elsie. "Guess it will be quite by the time I get home, with Rosie and Esther bangin' it round."

"I want my dolly! I want my dolly!" piped up little Isabel. "Where's my dolly?"

"Oh! may I get her the doll, Miss Lucy?" cried Elsie, running over to the chest of drawers where the ward's few playthings were kept.

Isabel trotted after, her face shining with expectation.

Barely waiting for the desired permission, Elsie dived down into the lower drawer, and, after a brief search among torn picture-books and odds and ends of broken toys, brought forth a little battered rubber doll, which had lost most of its coloring and all of its cry. But Baby Isabel hugged it to her heart, and at once dropped to the floor, crooning over her new treasure.

While the ward was thus discussing dolls,

Mrs. Jocelyn and Polly, downstairs, in the little lady's room, were conversing on the same subject.

It was Polly's first visit since the night she had sung to Burton Leonard, and they had talked of that and many other things.

"It is too bad for you to be shut up in a hospital all this beautiful summer," lamented Mrs. Jocelyn. "If I were only well, I'd carry you off home with me this very day, and we'd go driving out in the country, and have woodsy picnics, and all sorts of delightful things."

"I went to ride yesterday with Dr. Dudley," said Polly contentedly.

"Yes, that's all right as far as it goes; but your pleasures are too serious ones for the most part. You ought to be playing with dolls — without a care beyond them. By the way, I never have seen you with a doll yet."

"No, I haven't any," replied Polly sadly.

"But you have them up in the ward, don't you?"

"There's a little old rubber doll that

141

somebody left because it had n't any squeak — that's all."

"For pity's sake!" exclaimed the little lady. "The idea! — not a single doll that can be called a doll! I never heard anything like it! What do you play with? Or don't you play at all?"

"Oh, yes!" laughed Polly. "We play games, and Dr. Dudley has given me two story-books, and there are some toy soldiers — but they're 'most all broken now. Then there's a big book with pictures pasted in it — that's nice! There was a Noah's Ark; but a little boy threw Noah and nearly all the animals out of the window, and before we found them the rain spoiled some of them, and the rest were lost."

"I declare, it's pitiful!" sorrowed the little lady.

"Oh, we have a nice time!" smiled Polly.

"I believe you'd find something to enjoy on a desert, without a soul within fifty miles!" laughed Mrs. Jocelyn.

"Guess I'd be lonesome!" chuckled Polly. "But I always thought the sand would be lovely to play in."

"There, I told you so! Oh, you'd have a good time! But, child, have n't you any doll of your own — at home, I mean?"

"No, not now — I did have" — and pain crept into the sweet little face. "Mamma gave me a pretty doll the last Christmas — oh, I loved it so! But after I went to live with Aunt Jane I helped her 'most all the time I was out of school, and I did n't have much time to play with Phebe — she was named for mamma. Phebe was mamma's name. So finally Aunt Jane said that Maude might just as well have my doll. I felt as if I could n't give her up, but I had to —" Polly's lip quivered, and she swallowed hard.

"Poor little girl!" Mrs. Jocelyn put out a hand and gently stroked the bright curls. "How could anybody be so cruel!"

"I would n't have cared — much, if Maude had loved Phebe; but she did n't. She 'd swing her round by one leg, and pull her hair when she got mad, or — anything. It seemed as if I could n't stand it!"

"Bless you! I don't see how you could!" sympathized her listener.

"Why, I had to!" replied Polly simply.

143

"But one day — I never told anybody this, even Miss Lucy — one day Aunt Jane took the children to a circus, and I stayed home all alone. After they'd been gone about half an hour I went and dug as deep a hole as I could right in the middle of the clothes-yard — the woman upstairs was gone, too, so she could n't see me — and I wrapped Phebe up in a clean piece of paper, after I'd kissed her and bid her good-bye — and then I buried her! It 'most killed me to do it; but I could n't see any other way. Do you think it was dreadfully wicked?"

Polly looked up with wet, appealing eyes, and, to her amazement, saw that tears were running down the little lady's cheeks.

"Wicked!" Mrs. Jocelyn ejaculated. "If nobody ever did anything more wicked than that it would be a blessed sort of world! No, dearest; I'm glad you were brave enough to do it — as glad as can be! But what did they say when they came home? Did n't they miss the doll?"

"Not that night; they were so excited about the circus. They never said a word till some time the next morning; then Maude

144

wondered where Phebe was. I was dreadfully afraid they'd ask me if I knew; but Maude only looked for her a little while — she did n't love her a bit. Aunt Jane told her she was probably kicking round somewhere, and it served her right for not taking better care of her. I guess they forgot all about her pretty soon; but I did n't — I never shall forget Phebe!"

Mrs. Jocelyn put her arm around Polly, and held her close, murmuring sympathetic words, which were very comforting to the bereft little mother.

"How did Phebe look?" asked Mrs. Jocelyn, at last. "Do you want to tell me?"

"Oh, yes! She had light curly hair, just like mine, and such pretty blue eyes and red cheeks! She was about *so* tall," measuring a foot or more with her hands. "She had on a little white muslin dress, with blue sprigs on it — the other dresses Maude spoiled. She was just as sweet as she could be!" Polly's eyes almost brimmed over, and the lady gently led her thoughts to other things.

Soon Dr. Dudley came in, and then the little girl said good-bye.

On the stairs she heard her name called, and looking back she saw Miss Hortensia Price, a bunch of sweet peas in her hand.

"I was bringing these to you," the nurse smiled. "How do you do, my dear? Are you feeling quite well again?"

"Oh, yes, thank you!" cried Polly, her little nose among the flowers. "Doctor would n't let me get up day before yesterday, and now I'm so rested I don't feel as if I'd ever get tired."

"I am very glad. I meant to come up to see you sooner, but I did n't wish to disturb you that first day, and yesterday I was extremely busy."

"Burton is not worse, is he?" asked Polly quickly.

"Oh, no! he is doing even better than we anticipated. And at last he has decided to keep still — did Dr. Dudley tell you?"

"Yes," beamed Polly, "and I'm so glad!"

"We all are. He has been a hard child to manage. We have much to thank you for — I shall never forget what you have done!"

Polly was so astonished at this praise that

146

she could do nothing but blush and murmur a few words of dissent.

"Burton's mother," Miss Price went on, "wishes you would come in some time and sing her that hymn again, the last one you sang, 'The King of Love my Shepherd is.'"

"Oh," smiled Polly, "I wish she could hear David sing that! He sings it beautifully! I never heard it till that night, so I didn't know it very well; but if she could come up into the ward, I'm sure David would sing it for her."

Miss Price seemed to ignore David altogether, for she only said: —

"Polly May, if you can learn like that, with your sweet voice, — why, you must have a musical education! I shall speak to Dr. Dudley about it at once. But I'm keeping you standing here, child, and you not strong!"

Polly assured her that she was not tired in the least, and thanked her again for the flowers. Then she ran upstairs, to tell the astonishing news to Miss Lucy and the ward, and to show her sweet peas in proof of Miss Hortensia Price's wonderful kindness.

After everybody had had a sniff of the

fragrant blossoms, Polly proposed moving a little table to the side of David's cot, and placing the flowers on it.

"Because," she argued, "if David had n't sung the hymn that night, I could n't have, and if I had n't, maybe Miss Price would n't have given me the sweet peas; so I think they belong to David as much as to me."

The children — all but David, and his protests went for naught — accepted Polly's reasoning as perfectly logical, and readily helped carry out her suggestion. Miss Lucy smiled to herself, while she allowed them to do as they pleased.

"Will they keep till to-morrow, s'pose?" questioned Elsie anxiously.

"Of course," answered Polly. "Why?"

"'Cause they'll help celebrate," Elsie returned.

"Celebrate what?" queried Polly, wiping a drop of overrunning water from the glass which Miss Lucy had supplied.

"Why, the ward's birthday! Don't you know about it?" And Elsie looked her astonishment at having heard any news with which Polly was not already acquainted.

148

"I don't know what you mean," Polly replied.

Then what a babel of tongues! Each wanted to be first to inform Polly.

"The ward's five years old to-morrow!" — "Miss Lucy's been tellin' us!" — "It was started five years ago!" — "There was only three children in it then!" — "She said we ought to celebrate!" — "A lady give it to the hospital!"

"We'll every one wear a sweet pea all day!" announced Polly.

"That'll be lovely!" beamed Elsie.

"They'll wilt," objected practical Moses.

"Never mind!" returned Polly. "We can give 'em a drink once in a while."

So it was agreed. Meantime Miss Lucy, at her table, textbook in hand, overheard and wished and planned. Downstairs, too, where Mrs. Jocelyn sat talking with Dr. Dudley, more planning was going on, and in the physician's own heart a little private scheme was brewing. Thus the ward's birthday came nearer and more near.

The sweet peas were placed on a broad sill outside the window for the night, lest they might take it into their frail little heads to wither before their time. They showed their appreciation of Miss Lucy's thoughtfulness by being as sweet and bright as possible, and early in the morning everybody in the ward wore a decoration.

About ten o'clock Dr. Dudley appeared, and Polly and Elsie hurried to pin a posy in his buttonhole. Elsie had chosen a pink and Polly a blue blossom, and one little girl held them in place while the other pinned them fast, the Doctor sending telegraphic messages over their heads to Miss Lucy.

"Now, let me see," he began, after he had returned thanks for his sweets; "think I can squeeze in seven or eight of them?" nodding to the nurse.

"They're none of them very bulky," she laughed.

"Feel strong enough for an auto ride, Elsie?" he twinkled.

"Me?" gasped the little girl. "You don't mean me, do you?"

"If your name is Elsie Meyer, you're the one," he replied.

"Oh, my! O-h, m-y!" she cried. "Polly!

Polly! He's goin' to take me to ride!" And she whirled Polly round and round in her excited joy.

"Cornelius and Moses," he counted, "and Elsie and Polly," — his eyes had reached the little girl with a crutch, whose pale face was growing pink and paler by turns, — "and Leonora and Brida," he went on; "that makes six."

"Oh, me too?" squealed Brida delightedly, clutching her chair for support in the trying moment.

Leonora said nothing, only gazed at the Doctor as if she feared he would vanish, together with her promised ride, if she did not keep close watch.

"There are only two more for whom I dare risk the bumpety-bumps," laughed Dr. Dudley. "Corinne, I think you can bear them, and perhaps we can wedge in Isabel."

"Oh, we can hold her!" volunteered Elsie.

"Sure, we can!" echoed Cornelius.

"No, I want to thit in Polly'th lap," lisped the midget, edging away from the

151

others, and doing her best to climb to Polly's arms.

Polly clasped the tiny one tight, smiling her promise, too full of joy in her friends' happiness for any words.

"I'll give you fifteen minutes to prink up in," the Doctor told them; and away they scampered, Polly halting by David's cot long enough to wish he "were going too."

The eight were downstairs within the specified time, and they whirled off in the big motor car, which seated them all comfortably without crowding anybody. Very demure they were, passing along the city streets, but in the open country their delight found vent in shouts and squeals and jubilant laughter. Dr. Dudley chose a route apart from the traveled highways, leading through woods and between blossoming fields.

"Could we get out and pick just a few o' those flowers?" Elsie ventured; and presently they were all over the stone wall, Leonora with the rest, right down among the goldenrod and asters.

They went home with their arms full of beauty, too overjoyed even to guess that they had been away nearly two whole hours, and that it was dinner time.

Leonora was first to discover it — the beautiful copy of the Sistine Madonna, hanging opposite David's bed. Then dinner had to wait, while they flocked over to look at Dr. Dudley's gift to the ward.

"Why, it's just like a story," cried Elsie. "Something keeps happening all the time."

Miss Lucy smiled mysteriously, which made Polly wonder if there were more happenings in reserve for the day.

Dinner was barely cleared away when a rap sent Moses to the door. There stood one of the porters grinning behind a pyramid of white boxes tied with gay ribbons.

Moses was too astonished for anything but speechlessly to let the man pass him. The pile was deposited beside the nurse, and Elsie squealed out: —

"They look 'xac'ly like Christmas!"

"Perhaps the inside will look like Christmas, too," smiled Miss Lucy. "Let's see what this card says: —

153

"For the young folks of the Convalescent Ward, in honor of the Ward's fifth birthday. From Mrs. Juliet P. Jocelyn."

"This box is addressed to Miss Polly May;" and she handed out the one on top.

Polly received it with an "Oh, thank you!" A sudden tumultuous hope had sprung in her heart, and she gazed down at the oblong box with mingled anticipation and fear. What could it be but —! Yet what if it should n't be! With trembling fingers she hurriedly untied the blue ribbon. She hardly dared lift the cover; but — it was!

"Oh, Phebe!" she cried, with almost a sob, clasping the beautiful doll to her heart.

It was not Phebe, but so nearly like the cherished one it was not surprising in that first ecstatic moment Polly should think it was really her lost darling. Golden curls, blue eyes, and a frock of white muslin with blue sprigs made the resemblance very true. In her own bliss, Polly, for a minute, forgot her surroundings. Then she became suddenly aware that Elsie was dancing about,

154

shrieking with delight, holding a doll the counterpart of Polly's own, except for the color of dress and eyes.

Brida's doll had blue eyes, like the new Phebe, and Leonora's brown, like Elsie's.

Miss Lucy could not untie the boxes fast enough now, the children were so wildly excited. Every girl had a beautiful doll, and every boy a gift that made him shout in glee or wrapped him in speechless joy, according to his nature.

"How *did* she know I'd ruther have 'em than anything in th' biggest store you ever saw?" cried Cornelius, with a yell of rapture, throwing off the cover of his box to see a ball, a bat, and a catcher's mitt. "How did she, did she know it?"

The other big boys had similar presents and the younger lads mechanical toys of various kinds, — Railway and Track, Steamer, Automobile, Fire Engine, and a real little Flying Machine. Besides these there were a number of fascinating games and a box of stone blocks.

In the late afternoon some of the nurses made a brief visit, bringing their combined

155

gift, — a dozen books and a shelf to keep them on. Miss Price, who could not leave her patient, sent a set of crayons and outline picture-books to color. And so one delight followed another until the children were in a state of the happiest excitement.

Just before supper time Dr. Dudley came in, full of merriment and droll stories.

The tea was there on time, a regular "party tea," with a birthday cake and five small candles. The goodies seemed ready to be eaten; the little folks were eager to taste; still Miss Lucy did not give the word. She and the Doctor would turn towards the door at the slightest sound; then they would go on talking again. Finally Polly's sharp ears heard footsteps, approaching footsteps. Dr. Dudley listened, jumped up, and slipped outside the door, shutting it behind him. The steps drew nearer, there were low voices and faint laughter. Then something like a small commotion seemed to be taking place just outside. Elsie's impatience let loose her tongue.

"Oh, Miss Lucy! what is it? Do tell us! Please do!"

"In a minute there'll be no need of telling," was the smiling answer.

At the instant a light rap sent Polly and Elsie flying to the door. Polly was ahead, and threw it wide open on a pretty picture, — little Mrs. Jocelyn seated in a wheel chair, Dr. Dudley and a porter in the background.

"Oh, o-h!" cried Polly, "how perfectly lovelicious!" And she stepped aside to let the guest roll herself in.

Miss Lucy came forward with a glad greeting, while the flock of girls and boys retreated, struck with sudden shyness.

Polly laid hold of Elsie and Leonora. "Come!" she whispered. "Come, and shake hands with her!"

"No, no! I can't!" gasped Leonora, terrified at thought of speaking to that beautiful little white-haired lady in the exquisite gray silk.

"Yes, come!" urged Polly. "She gave us our dolls, and we must thank her!" Her hand on Leonora's gave the timid girl courage, and she allowed herself to be led towards the wheel chair.

They were all presented by name, and

157

Mrs. Jocelyn won the girls' hearts with kisses and kindly words, while the boys, from Cornelius O'Shaughnessy to little John Fritz, were so charmed by her interest in their sports that they afterwards voted her "a dandy one" — their highest praise.

The tea went off, as all party teas ought to go, to the music of merry laughter; and when the ice cream came on, the children's glee reached its height — it was in the form of quaint little girls and boys!

It was nearly bedtime when the last gift arrived. The parcel was oblong and flat and heavy.

"I bet it's another picture!" ventured Moses.

Polly fairly shouted when Miss Lucy folded back the wrappings. There lay a superb photograph, handsomely framed in oak, of Lone Star and his master. This note accompanied it: —

To the Children's Convalescent Ward:

DEAR WARD: — News has just come that you are having a birthday. I congratulate you on having lived and prospered for five

158

long years. As I have counted only four birthdays myself, I have great respect for those that have attained to five.

I cannot let the day pass without sending you a small token of neighborly affection, and because the hour is late and I have nothing better in sight I trust you will pardon my seeming egotism in presenting my own picture.

With bushels of joyful wishes for your future, I will sign myself

Your fast friend,

LONE STAR.

CHAPTER XI

POLLY PLAYS THE PART OF EVA

SUMMER still lingered, but signs were abroad of her coming departure. Noons were hot, and nights were chill; bird carols were infrequent; chrysanthemums were unfurling their buds. The vines that festooned the windows of the children's convalescent ward sent an occasional yellow-coated messenger to the lilac bushes below — a messenger that never came back.

Inside the ward there were even greater changes. Of the old set of summer patients only a few remained to keep Polly company. Elsie and Brida, Corinne and Isabel, with Moses and Cornelius, had received their discharge and had returned to their homes. Leonora stayed for more of the treatment that was slowly lessening her lameness and her pain. David had so far recovered as to have been appointed office boy for Dr. Dudley, a position which was, according to David's version, "all pay and no work." But somebody was needed to answer telephone calls during the physician's absence, as well as to note any messages that might arrive for him, and David's strength was now sufficient for the service. So the arrangement was proving a very happy one, and was especially enjoyed by Polly and Leonora.

As their acquaintances drifted away from the hospital, and strangers drifted in, these three became close friends. The girls would join David in the office, generally bringing their dolls with them, when David would be the one to tell or read a story, for his aunt kept him well supplied with interesting tales. Sometimes, especially in the early twilight hour, Dr. Dudley was story-teller; or more often they would talk over together the happenings of the day, the children unconsciously gathering from the physician's rich store bits of wisdom that would abide with them as long as memory lived.

They were watching for him, one night, when the telephone bell rang.

David sprang to answer the call, and the girls heard him say: —

"No, sir, he is not in. — He went out about an hour ago. — We expect him every minute now. — Yes, sir, I will."

The boy came back looking a little excited.

"It was Uncle David!" he told them. "He says he is sick, and he wants Dr. Dudley to come over."

"Oh, dear," scowled Polly; "I hope there isn't anything bad the matter with him!"

"It is the first time I ever spoke to him," said David slowly. "But, of course, he didn't know it was I that was talking."

"There's the Doctor!" cried Leonora, as a runabout stopped at the entrance.

"Shall I go tell him?" and Polly started.

But the lad was already on his way.

"Let me, please!" he answered. "I want to do that much for Uncle David."

"I thought it might tire him to go fast," murmured Polly, apologetically, as she joined Leonora at the window.

"He'll get all out of breath!" worried Leonora. "Just see him run!"

"He isn't thinking of himself," Polly responded. "It's just like him! But his heart

162

is pretty strong now, I guess. Though Doctor told him to be careful."

David returned a little pale, and Polly made him lie down on the couch.

He did not seem inclined to talk, and the girls waited at the window, conversing in low tones over their dolls. By and by Dr. Dudley came up the walk, and Polly ran to open the door for him.

The physician acknowledged the attention with a grave smile, and then went directly to the telephone, calling for Miss Batterson.

David sat up. The girls listened breathlessly.

Presently they heard arrangements being made for the nurse to go to the Colonel at once, and they gathered from what was said that David's great-uncle was ill with typhoid fever, and that the Doctor had ordered him to bed.

"He has kept up too long," regretted Dr. Dudley, as he hung the receiver on its hook. "As it is he'll have to go through a course of fever. He is furious at the prospect, but it can't be helped."

"I'm so sorry," mourned Polly.

Then, seeing that there was no likelihood of a story or even talk from the Doctor, she proposed, softly to Leonora, that they go upstairs.

"No, stay here with David, if you wish; you're not in the way. I'm going back with Miss Batterson."

So they remained, while the physician put some medicines in his case, and gave David directions regarding a probable caller.

Soon the nurse came in, suit case in hand, and the two went off together.

"I hope mother won't hear of it right away," the lad mused. "She thinks so much of Uncle David. She'd want to go and do something for him, you know, and she could n't, and so she'd worry."

Polly recalled her recent drive through Forest Park, and could scarcely realize that the big, strong man who had made the time so pleasant for her was now weak and miserable from disease.

David related incidents of his mother's life with her uncle when she was a small girl, one leading to another, until, suddenly, Dr. Dudley opened the door.

"What!" he exclaimed. "My girlies not abed yet! Why, it is nearly nine o'clock! Miss Lucy will think I have kidnaped you."

They hurried away, with laughing good-nights, after being assured by the Doctor that probably Colonel Gresham would "come out all right."

David slept downstairs now, in a tiny room adjoining the physician's, and his last thought that night was of the strangeness of it all — Uncle David's hurrying to catch Dr. Dudley for him, and his being the first to notify the Doctor of his uncle's illness, while they had not even a bowing acquaintance with each other!

For a few days there was no alarming change in Colonel Gresham's condition. Then he grew worse. He became delirious, and remained so, recognizing no one. The anxiety felt in Dr. Dudley's office extended upstairs to the little people of the convalescent ward, for since the Colonel's birthday gift they had taken great interest in the master of the famous trotter. Every morning they were eager for the latest news from the second house away where their friend lay so ill.

The twentieth of September was hot and oppressive. Early in the evening thunder clouds heaped the western sky, and occasional flashes of lightning portended a shower.

After the children were established for the night, Miss Lucy sat long by the open window watching the electrical display. The clouds rose slowly, lingering beyond the western hills with no wind to aid their progress. Finally she partly undressed, and throwing on a kimono settled herself comfortably upon her cot, to await the uncertain storm, ready to shut the windows in case of driving rain. By and by fitful breezes fluttered through the room, the low rumbling of thunder was heard, and presently a soft patter of drops on the leaves. The lightning grew brilliant. The nurse dreamed and waked by turns. At length she was aroused by steps along the corridor. They sounded like Dr. Dudley's. She was at the door as the physician's knuckle touched it. In response to his voice she stepped outside, that they might not disturb the sleepers.

"I want to take Polly over to Colonel Gresham's," the Doctor explained. "He keeps on calling for 'Eva,' and nothing will quiet him. He is on the verge of collapse."

"Did n't Mrs. Collins come?"

"Yes; but he did n't know her. It broke her all up. I think now that he has gone back to the time when she was a little girl, and possibly has confounded her with Polly. At any rate, I'm going to try the experiment of taking Polly over. It can do no harm, and may do some good."

The hall suddenly burst into light, and there was a simultaneous roar of thunder.

"We're going to have a shower," observed the Doctor.

"I should think it was already here," returned Miss Lucy. "Had n't you better wait till it passes, before taking Polly out?"

"Oh, no! Wrap her up well, and I'll carry her. It is only a few steps; she won't get wet."

Polly was a quaint little figure in the long mackintosh, and it tripped her feet once or twice, until the Doctor drew it from her and threw it across his arm.

167

The thunder had been lighter for some minutes; but as they halted at the entrance before going out a tremendous crash jarred the building.

"Not afraid, Thistledown?" smiled Dr. Dudley, as he wrapped her again in the long cloak.

"I don't like it," she confessed; "but I shan't mind with you," putting her arms around his neck.

The rain was pouring as they left the piazza, and before they were off the grounds big stones of hail were pelting their umbrella. The Doctor hurried along, the lightning glaring about them and the air filled with thunder.

Colonel Gresham's house was nearly reached, when a sudden gust turned the umbrella, and almost at once came a blaze of light and a terrific crash — a great oak across the street had been split from top to root!

With a gasp of terror Polly clung to the Doctor's neck, and he sped up the walk on a quick run.

"There!" he exclaimed, setting her down

inside the door, "you're safe and sound! But next time we'll take Miss Lucy's advice, and not run any such risks."

"It was awful, wasn't it?" breathed Polly.

"A little too close for comfort," he smiled, taking her wet coat and spreading it over a chair.

At the foot of the stairs he halted for a few instructions.

"Humor the Colonel in every way possible," he told Polly. "If he names you 'Eva,' let him think he is right, and call him 'Uncle David.'"

"I'm afraid I shall make a mistake," replied Polly.

"You won't," he assured her. "Just imagine you are his little niece, doing everything to please him — that is all."

Miss Batterson smiled down on Polly, as she entered the sick-room, and spoke in a low voice to the physician.

Colonel Gresham had been muttering indistinctly, and now broke into his persistent call: —

"Eva! Eva! Where's Eva?"

Dr. Dudley gave Polly a gentle push towards the bed.

"Here I am, Uncle David!" she answered, standing where the light slanted across her yellow curls.

The sick man started up, and then dropped back on his pillow.

"Oh, you've come!" he cried, with a breath of relief. "Why did you stay away — so — long?"

"I did n't know you wanted me till now, Uncle David," replied the soft voice.

"Come nearer, child! Let me feel your little hand! I dreamed — I dreamed — you were gone — forever!"

He lay quiet for a moment, her cool fingers in his hot, trembling palm. Then he startled her by the sudden cry: —

"That water! It's dripping, dripping right on my head! Eva, put up your hand, and catch it!"

Standing beside his pillow, Polly held her hand high.

"I'll catch it all, Uncle David," she assured him. "You shan't feel another drop!"

170

"That's a good girl! You always are a good girl, Eva! Seems as — if —"

The voice trailed off into confused mutterings, and with trembling fingers he began picking at the sheet and working it into tiny rolls.

Very gently Polly took one of the restless hands in both her own, and smoothed it tenderly.

This had a quieting effect, and he lay still for so long that Dr. Dudley drew Polly softly away, letting her rest on his knee, her head against his shoulder.

But in a moment the old call burst out: —
"Eva! Eva! Where are you, Eva?"

Her prompt assurance, "I'm right here, Uncle David!" hushed him at once. Presently, however, he began again.

"Eva! Eva! You love your old uncle, don't you, Eva? Just a — little — bit?"

"More than a little bit! I love you dearly, Uncle David!"

"Don't go away any more! Promise, Eva! Promise me!"

"I'll stay just as long as you want me, Uncle David. Can't you go to sleep? Remember, I'll be right here all the time!"

171

Reassured by this, he closed his eyes, and was quiet for a while; yet only to rouse again and repeat the same old cry.

The thunder was now only an occasional rumble in the distance, and the lightning had faded to a glimmer; but the rain still kept on, and as the nurse raised another window the ceaseless patter of the drops seemed to disturb the sick man, for he began his complaint of the dripping water upon his head.

Polly pacified him, as before, and once more he drowsed.

The little girl slept, too, in the Doctor's arms, until, towards morning the Colonel was resting so calmly that they returned to the hospital.

Miss Lucy clasped Polly with almost a sob.

"If you ever go away again in such a storm," she declared, "I shall go, too! I saw the lightning come down — and —" her voice broke.

"And we were not harmed in the least," finished the Doctor cheerily. "But next time I promise to act upon your higher wisdom, and not venture among such thunder-

172

bolts. Now, hustle into bed, both of you, and don't dare to wake up till breakfast time!"

The convalescent ward slept late; the nurse and Polly strictly obeyed orders. Nobody cared, however, and unusual gayety prevailed at the tardy breakfast, to match the bright September morning and the good news of Colonel Gresham. For word had come up from Dr. Dudley that the Colonel was going to get well.

Of course the children eagerly heard the story of Polly's midnight trip in the physician's arms through the fearful storm. It had to be told over and over again, and the more daring ones wished they had been awake to see it all.

The details of what had taken place in the sick-room Polly wisely withheld; but the girls and boys were undoubtedly more interested in the account of the lightning's striking the familiar big oak tree than they would have been in the more important part of that night's strange story.

It was not many weeks afterward that Dr. Dudley brought Polly a message.

173

"The Colonel says he feels slighted because you don't come to see him, and I promised to send you over."

"Oh, I shall love to go!" cried Polly. "I'll run right off and change my dress."

Colonel Gresham was in a great chair by the window, and begged his small guest's pardon for not rising to greet her.

"I'm not quite firm on my legs yet," he laughed, "and I must n't topple over, as Miss Batterson has left me for a whole hour."

"Oh, then I'll stay and wait on you!" beamed Polly. "And if you get tired hearing me talk, you can go to sleep."

But the Colonel seemed very wide awake, and after a gay chat he began: —

"Dr. Dudley has been telling me about bringing you over here in that thunderstorm, and how you quieted me when nobody else could."

"Yes," replied Polly innocently, "you thought I was your little niece, Eva, and — "

"What?" broke in her listener, amazement in his tone.

"Oh, I s'posed he 'd told you!" cried Polly, in dismay. "I ought not to have — "

174

"Yes, you ought!" he interrupted. "What did I say?"

Polly hesitated. She was not at all sure that Dr. Dudley would wish her to disclose the wanderings of the Colonel's mind, since he had not done so himself. But there seemed no other way, so she replied simply: —

"Oh, you did n't say much! Only you kept calling for Eva, and so I pretended I was she, and I called you Uncle David. And you heard the rain, and thought it was dripping on your head, and you wanted me to hold my hand up to catch it. That was about all."

Polly cast furtive glances at the Colonel. She could make nothing of his face, beyond that it was very grave. She wondered if he were displeased with her.

After a time he spoke.

"You have done me a kindness that can never be repaid. Such debts cannot be balanced with money. So we won't talk about pay. But I should like to do something for you — give you a sort of remembrance. I don't know what would make you happiest;

175

but you may chose, 'to the half of my kingdom' — anything but Lone Star. I'm afraid
I should hate to give up Lone Star!"

Polly laughed, and the Colonel laughed
too, which put the talk on a cheery footing,
and she assured him that she should n't have
chosen Lone Star anyway, because she did
n't know how to take care of a horse, and
had n't any place to keep him in.

Then her face grew suddenly serious, and
she sat gazing at the pattern of the rug so
long that Colonel Gresham smiled to himself.

"Is it too much of a problem?" he finally
asked. "Can't you think of anything within
my power that would give you a little happiness?"

"Oh, yes!" Polly answered quickly; "but
I'm afraid —" she stopped.

"Afraid of what?" he questioned.

"Afraid it is too much to ask," she replied
softly, lifting her thoughtful eyes to his.

"No, it is n't! Anything that will add to
your happiness —"

"Oh, this would make me very happy!"

"Out with it then! 'To the half of my
kingdom,' remember!"

176

"And you won't be offended?"

"I give you my word," he smiled.

"Well," she began slowly, "I should like best of all to have you — oh, I wish you would forgive David's mother, and love her again! She loves you so much!"

For several minutes — it seemed an hour to Polly — the marble clock over the fireplace, with the bronze mother and child sitting there, tick-tocked its way uninterruptedly. The little girl did not dare to look up. Her heart beat very fast indeed. It hurt her to breathe. Had she made Colonel Gresham so angry that he would never speak to her again? She wondered how long it would be before she could gain enough courage for just one glance at his face. Then he spoke.

"You have given me a hard task, little Polly! It would be easier to go through the fever again!" His voice was gentle — very gentle, but sad.

"Oh, please, please excuse me!" she exclaimed earnestly. "I ought not to have asked it! I'll take it all back! You said what would make me happiest — and so — and so —" She put her face down in her

177

hands. "I did n't mean to hurt you!" she sobbed, "I did n't! I did n't!"

"Child! child! this will never do! It is I who am wholly to blame! You have done nothing to excuse. I shall keep my promise to you, if you are sure that what you have asked will give you the greatest happiness."

He waited for her answer — Polly never guessed with what selfish longing.

Her face burst into radiance.

"Oh, will you!" she exclaimed. "It will make me so happy, happy, I shan't know what to do!"

Colonel Gresham was very pale, but Polly did not notice. She was looking through rose-colored glasses.

"Is David still at the hospital?" the Colonel inquired.

"Yes, sir; he stays in Dr. Dudley's office now, to answer the telephone and attend to things. He 's almost well."

"Well enough to walk over here, think?"

"Oh, yes, sir!" Polly beamed.

"Suppose you run and fetch him then. Say to him that I should like to make his acquaintance."

178

Polly needed no urging for such a bliss-ful errand, and in her excitement failed to hear the Doctor's approaching footsteps. At the threshold she nearly ran into his arms.

"Why such haste, Thistledown? Have you and Colonel Gresham quarreled?"

"Oh, no! I'm going after David. Do you care if he leaves the office for just a little while?"

"Certainly not. Tell him from me that he can come."

If the Doctor felt any surprise, neither his voice nor his face showed it.

It cost Polly a deal of talk to convince David that his uncle had actually sent for him, and then, after he had said that he would go, he was afraid that his clothes were not just right for such a visit.

"Never mind your clothes!" cried Polly. "He'll never know what you have on."

"Well, I must brush my hair," delayed the boy, dreading the ordeal before him.

"Oh, your hair's well enough! Don't flat it down! It's so pretty as it is now — all curly and fluffy!"

179

So they were finally started, Polly talking so fast that David had small chance for nervousness or fear.

Dr. Dudley was not in sight when the children entered Colonel Gresham's room, and Polly made a silent wild guess regarding his speedy going away. To David's pleasure the Colonel received him as he would have received any other lad whom Polly had brought for a call. There was no reference to his mother or to their kinship, and the boy began at once to feel at ease. He inquired about his recent injury and his stay at the hospital, and then, by a chance remark of Polly's, the subject of David's church singing was brought up.

Conversation had not begun to flag, when Polly spied the Doctor's auto at the curb. Mrs. Collins was stepping out!

David's sentence broke off square in the middle; but Colonel Gresham did not appear to notice. Footsteps neared the door, and the children sat breathless; yet the Colonel still talked on as quietly as before.

When the door opened, Polly saw his fingers grip the arms of his chair. His voice faltered off into silence.

Dr. Dudley stepped aside, and David's mother appeared on the threshold, a little slight, fair-haired woman, her face now pink with emotion, her eyes big and shining.

The Colonel held out both hands; there was a swish of skirts and something like a sob.

Polly heard, "Eva!" — "Oh, Uncle David!" Then she slipped out to the Doctor, and he softly shut the door.

They went downstairs hand in hand, and so to the street.

"We'll have a little ride," he proposed, "to let off steam. There aren't any patients that will hurt by waiting."

The car passed slowly up the pleasant street.

"Thistledown," he said tenderly, "you have accomplished a blessed work this morning."

"Why," exclaimed Polly, in surprise, "I have n't done a single thing — only go after David! It's the Colonel that's done it all!

But is n't it splendid of him? Are n't you glad for David?"

"I am glad for them all. It is what I feared never would come to pass. Colonel Gresham is sure to like David, and it is going to mean everything for the boy."

CHAPTER XII

THE KIDNAPING OF POLLY

MAMMA and I are going to live with Uncle David." So the boy told Polly late that afternoon. "He says he has lost time enough, and now we must come as soon as we can pack up."

"Isn't that splendid!" beamed Polly, thinking she had never seen David look so happy or so handsome.

"Uncle David is nicer — a great deal nicer — than I dreamed he could be. O Polly, I can't thank you enough!"

"Thank me?" repeated Polly. "What for?"

"Polly May!" and David gazed at her incredulously. Then he laughed.

"Oh, you little bunch of unselfishness!" he cried. "I believe you haven't the least idea that Uncle David's making up with us is all your doing!"

"Why, David Collins, it isn't! I just told

him it would make me happy if he would —
that's all!"

"Just as I said!" he laughed. "O Polly,
Polly! don't you see — no, no, I'd rather you
would n't! Don't try to see!"

"I could n't!" chuckled Polly. "There
is n't anything to see!"

"All right! It's grand anyway! Mamma
looks so much prettier and younger! Oh, you
can't think how happy —"

The telephone cut off his sentence, and he
ran across the office.

He listened a moment; then Polly heard
him say, "She is right here. If you'll wait,
please, I'll ask her."

David turned from the instrument. "It is
Mrs. Jocelyn," he explained. "She wants
you to come up there to-morrow afternoon,
and stay all night and next day. Her cousin's little girl — Dorothy Cannon, I think
the name is — will be there, and she wants
you too."

"Oh, of course I'll go!" and Polly's eyes
shone: "that is, if Miss Lucy or Dr. Dudley don't need me for anything, and I don't
suppose they will. Tell her I'll come, unless

they do. Oh, and, David,"—for he had taken up the receiver again,—"ask her what time she wants me, please!"

He gave the message, and then turned back to Polly.

"She says to come as early as you can after dinner. Dear me, it will be awfully lonesome without you!"

"It will, won't it?" Polly's face sobered. "But then," she brightened, "you'll have to be home helping your mother pack up, shan't you?"

"So I shall," he returned. "And it will be a good time for you to go. Ever hear of this Dorothy before?"

"Oh, yes! Mrs. Jocelyn has told me lots about her. I guess she's nice. She's twelve."

"You'll have a fine time, and I'll try to be glad you're going," laughed David.

Polly danced off to tell Miss Lucy and Leonora of her invitation, waving a gay good-bye to David from the doorway. She had made several visits of a day to Mrs. Jocelyn, who had left the hospital some weeks before; but she had never remained

185

overnight. And to see the Dorothy Cannon of whom she had heard so many happy things! She went upstairs on tiptoe of anticipation.

Miss Lucy was pleased, and Leonora tried to be. Polly saw through her forced smiles, however, and proposed all the pleasant make-ups she could think of.

"You can take care of Phebe while I'm gone, and play she's twin sister to your Juliet" (Leonora had named her doll after its donor), "and you may take the book Burton Leonard sent me. We have n't read more than half the stories in it yet."

Leonora was beaming her thanks and her delight, when Miss Lucy declared that she should depend on her to help entertain the ward, and that made her look so joyful, Polly knew there would be little lonesomeness for the lame girl.

When Dr. Dudley heard that Polly was going, he promised to carry her in his automobile, for it was a long walk to Mrs. Jocelyn's home.

"Then I shall have you to myself a little longer than the rest of them," he twinkled.

186

"Anybody'd think I was n't ever coming back!" laughed Polly.

"Oh, don't say so!" shivered Leonora. "Talk about what you're going to wear!"

"All right!" Polly agreed. "Miss Lucy and I have got it all planned. I shall wear my best white dress, if it is as warm as it is to-day, and take my white sweater with me, so I'll have it if it comes off cold. And I'm going to wear my beautiful locket and chain that Mrs. Leonard gave me, and my newest blue hair ribbon, and my best ties, and my best hat."

"Dear me," mused Dr. Dudley gravely, "I did n't know I should have to sit beside so fine a young lady as that! I wonder if I must put on my dress suit."

Polly giggled, and Leonora squealed, and they were not sobered down when they bade the Doctor good-night.

"Is n't he nice?" admired the lame girl, as they went slowly upstairs, hand in hand.

"He's the very nicest man in the whole world!" asserted Polly, and her nodding curls emphasized her praise.

Dressing came directly after dinner, and

187

Polly had the eager assistance of every girl in the ward that was able to be about on two feet.

Angiola Cuneo fetched the pretty black ties, and Mabel Camp the long stockings. Frederica Schmelzer held the box containing the hair ribbon of delicate blue while Miss Lucy brushed the fluffy curls into smoothness. Stella Pope, greatly puffed up by the importance of her errand, went to Miss Lucy's own room, and brought back the dainty white frock, all spotless from the laundry. But Leonora's was the crowning service of all. With trembling fingers she clasped around Polly's white neck the exquisite little gold chain, with its pendent locket, which had been Mrs. Leonard's farewell gift when Burton left the hospital.

"There," she whispered delightedly, patting Polly's shoulder, "you look too sweet for anything!"

Polly dimpled and blushed, but only said: —

"I wish you were going, too!"

"Oh my!" gasped Leonora; "I should n't

know how to act or what to say! I guess I'd rather stay with Miss Lucy."

The nurse, gathering up some of Polly's tossed-off belongings, smiled comfortably to herself, overhearing Leonora's words. She rarely had so much as to hint a reproof to Polly for any breach of courtesy; the child seemed instinctively to know what was due to others. She could be trusted anywhere without a fear.

The auto was waiting at the curb, Dr. Dudley and Polly were on their way from office to entrance, when there came a hurried call for the Doctor from one of his patients in a private ward.

"That's too bad!" he ejaculated. "I wish she had put off her attack an hour. Now you'll have to walk — or wait, and it is uncertain how soon I shall be at liberty."

"Oh, I don't mind walking!" smiled Polly.

"Well, here's for a good time, Thistledown!" And the Doctor kissed her on both cheeks.

She watched him up the stairs, and then went out alone.

189

"I wish I could have had the ride with him," she sighed, as she passed the inviting auto; "but it's a lovely day for a walk," she added. "I shall be there before I know it."

She waved her hand to Miss Lucy and the children, up at the window, who looked astonished to see her walking. Laughing at their surprise, she flourished her sweater and the little bundle containing her nightgown. Then shrubbery hid them from view. As she went by Colonel Gresham's, she wondered how soon David would be living there. Today he was at home, helping his mother, as she had predicted he might be.

A full third of the distance was passed, when, turning a corner, she met a tall woman in a brown skirt and white waist.

"Wh —," she gasped; "Aunt Jane!"

The woman gave a short laugh.

"You did n't expect to see me; did you? Where you bound for, all rigged out so fine?"

"I'm going to Mrs. Jocelyn's," Polly answered faintly.

"What! that rich Mrs. Jocelyn?"

"I guess so."

190

"Where does she live?"

"Up on Edgewood Avenue."

"Yes, that's the one," nodded the other. "You are comin' on! I s'pose you don't go to see anybody but millionaires now'days! You hain't been down to my house in an age."

"Mrs. Jocelyn was at the hospital," Polly explained, "and she's invited me up to stay all night, because her cousin's coming."

"Well, I was on my way to see you and take you home with me. Glad you happened along, for it will save my climbin' that hill. Here I am slavin' myself to death, and you're kitin' off hither and yon just to have a good time. I thought you was goin' to help 'em out at the hospital."

"I do help all I can," Polly put in meekly.

"Looks like it! Well, come on! I've got a pile o' work waitin' for me at home. Much as ever I could get away anyhow."

Polly stepped forward, and the two walked along together.

"I thought you'd come over and see your new uncle, even if you did n't care anything about me and your cousins."

191

"My new uncle?" repeated Polly, looking puzzled.

The woman laughed. "Did n't you hear I'd got married again?" she asked.

"Why, no!" cried Polly.

"I was married three weeks ago to-day," was the proud announcement. "He's got a good job at the Silver Plate, and I'm takin' work from the button fact'ry; so we're gittin' on. We've moved over on Chestnut Street — got a flat now. The kids think it's fine."

"I'm glad, Aunt Jane," Polly managed to say, just as she reached the street which led out in the direction of Edgewood Avenue. "I have to go this way." She stepped back to allow her aunt to pass on.

"Well, I guess not much!" and the child's arm was gripped by a strong hand. "You're goin' home with me — that's what!"

"Oh, not to-day!" cried Polly, in sudden terror. "I can't, Aunt Jane! I've promised to go up to Mrs. Jocelyn's!"

"That don't make any difference! You can go up there some other time — or you can stay away, just as I choose to have you!

192

Now, you need n't go to cryin' and makin' a fuss!" for Polly's lip was quivering. "I guess you know me well enough to know that when I set out to do a thing I do it, and this afternoon I said I was goin' to fetch you home, and I expect to keep my word."

A wild thought of flight swept through Polly's mind; but she at once realized how futile would be an attempt to run away. Her arm was still held as in a vise, and she was being led along an unfamiliar street. Aunt Jane nodded now and then to people they met, and could quickly call any number to her assistance. Polly decided that this was no time for escape.

"Where'd you get that locket and chain?" her captor queried.

"They were a present from Mrs. Leonard."

"What Mis' Leonard?"

"I don't know. Her little boy was sick at the hospital, and I sung —"

"Oh, that one! Mis' Marvin Leonard it is. Well, they'd ought to given you some money, too — they've got enough. I read in

the paper about your singin' — and faintin'
away."

"In the newspaper?" Polly's face showed
her astonishment.

"Sure! Did n't you know it? I should
think some o' them doctors or nurses might
have let you see the piece. And they'd ought
to had your picture taken to go along with
it."

"Oh, no!" breathed Polly shrinkingly.

"Huh! you're a great kid! Folks round
here thought it was a pretty smart thing.
You hain't no call to be ashamed of it."

The little girl attempted no reply. She
felt that Aunt Jane would not understand.

Arrived on the fourth floor of the big
tenement house, Polly was at once called
upon to praise the new quarters.

"Ain't this more swell than that old-
fashioned rent on Brewery Street?"

"Yes, I guess it is," was the rather doubtful response, for Polly, in her swift survey of
the narrow, gaudy parlor, discerned little to
admire.

"I s'pose it ain't much compared to the
elegance of your millionaire friends," Aunt

194

Jane flung out, nettled at the child's lack of approval.

"Mrs. Jocelyn's furniture is very plain — if you mean her," replied Polly gently.

"Well, come in here and put your things," leading the way to a little dim bedroom, lighted only from the apartment in front. "Better take off that white dress, and keep it clean; I'll get you one of Sophia's to wear till I can send for your clothes."

Slowly and sadly Polly laid aside her hat, and began to unbutton her dainty frock. Tears welled up in her eyes, at thoughts of Miss Lucy; but with a mighty effort she winked them back.

"There! — try that, and see how it fits."

Aunt Jane had emerged from the depths of a dark closet, and now tossed a limp calico print towards Polly.

The child could discern soiled patches on front and sleeves, and she revolted against the unclean garment; but silently she put it on.

"Well, that ain't so bad!" approved Aunt Jane. "Sophia's a whole year younger than you; but she takes a bigger waist. Stand out there — my, but it's short! Never mind! here's a petticoat to go with it."

Polly looked down in dismay. She had thought she might perhaps steal away to the hospital, just to let the Doctor and Miss Lucy know where she was; but she could never brave the street in such a skirt.

"Now I'll go to sewin' buttons, and you can do up the dinner dishes. I left 'em, thinkin' you'd be here. This is the way to the kitchen." And presently Polly found herself in a little stuffy box of a room, with a tableful of greasy dishes before her.

"Where are the children?" she ventured.

"At school, of course, — where you ought to be. Marcus and 'Melie I left at Mis' Cobbe's. That Marcus is a terror! I shall be thankful when he goes to school. Why did n't they send you this fall? You'll be 'way back in your books."

"Dr. Dudley has made arrangements for me to go to a school near the hospital; it does n't begin till next week."

"Oh, a private school! My, if they ain't puttin' the airs on to you!"

"It's near. That's why —"

196

"Huh! Well, 't ain't near here. I guess you can git along with the one my kids go to."

Polly did not reply. Experience had taught her to be sparing of words with Aunt Jane. She was still toiling with the heavy crockery, when a rush of feet in the hallway announced that school was out.

The door banged wide.

"Hoh! you've got back, have yer?"

"Hullo, Poll!"

"Say, what you wearin' my dress for?"

"Oh, you've got on a gold locket! Le' me see it!" Katie's fingers began pulling at the clasp.

"Oh, don't, please!" cried Polly. "I'll unfasten it for you as soon as I get the dishes done."

"I want to see it now! Mamma, shan't Polly take off her locket, and let me see it?"

"Polly, why can't you try to please your cousin, and not be so stingy with your things?"

"My hands are soapy," she apologized, "and —"

"Well, don't you know enough to wipe

them?" snapped Aunt Jane. "You seem to have grown very helpless."

"Say, what are these blue stones in here?" queried Katie, turning the locket curiously.

"Turquoises," Polly answered, eyeing with fear Katie's rough handling.

"Whose picture is this?" was the next question. "Stop, you Gregory — you'll break it! Mamma, shan't he stop pulling it so?"

"Yes, Gregory, you just wait, like a good boy, till your sister's seen it; then you can take it."

Polly trembled. Her beautiful locket and chain in Gregory's dirty fingers!

"You have n't told me who this is," complained Katie.

"Burton Leonard."

"It's the kid she sung to," added the mother; "the one the paper told about."

"Oh!" cried Katie. "What big eyes he's got!" And she snapped the locket together.

"Now it's my turn!" asserted Maude, snatching the pretty thing from her sister's hand.

Gregory burst into a wail.

198

"Yer said I could have it next!" he lamented.

"Let him take it!" urged the mother. But Maude only clasped the chain about her own neck, and danced off to the looking-glass over the sink.

"Yer mean old thing!" screamed Gregory.

"Come get it, Greg!" Sophia darted towards her sister.

"When yer do, let me know!" jeered Maude, eluding their outstretched hands, and putting a chair between them and herself.

A short skirmish was followed by a chase around the room, until their mother interposed.

"Gracious me! what a hubbub! Maude Simpson, bring that locket to me this minute!"

"It wasn't my fault at all!" whimpered Maude, taking off the chain and dropping it in her mother's lap.

"There's never no peace when you kids are in the house!" grumbled the woman, tossing aside her work, and disappearing in the next room.

"What yer done with it?" whined Gregory, as she came back with empty hands.

"I've put it where you won't find it in a hurry," she answered tartly. "Now hustle outdoors, the whole of you, and don't show your heads in here again till supper time!"

Polly drew a breath of relief, as the last Simpson vanished. She had forgotten how turbulent the children were.

When the dishes were out of the way began Polly's first lesson in sewing buttons to cards, and to Aunt Jane's delight she could soon do the work quickly and well.

"You'll be quite a help," was the commendation that brought a little solace to her sore heart. "Thank goodness, you're quieter than my own kids!"

So passed the afternoon, until came supper and the new uncle.

Polly had been helping set the table, when the door opened, and a little, thin-featured man stepped softly in.

"Polly May, I'll make you acquainted with your Uncle 'Rastus, 'Rastus Bean," called Aunt Jane from the cupboard that served for china closet and pantry.

"How do you do, my dear? How do you do?" smiled Mr. Erastus Bean, holding out his hand. "I'm very glad to see you."

Polly's little fingers had barely touched the strong, wiry ones, when Mrs. Bean's rasping voice broke in.

"Come along and wash up, 'Rastus! The water's good and hot."

Polly's hand was dropped, as if it had been of the temperature of the water.

"Yis, I'm comin', Jane! I'm comin' fas' 's I can!" The little man hurried across to the sink.

The children tumbled in, Gregory sprawling across the threshold and knocking Katie against a chair.

"Why don't yer ever look where yer goin'?" fretted Sophia.

"He's always runnin' over me!" wailed Katie.

"Say, where's Marcus and 'Melie?" demanded Maude.

"Over to Mis' Cobbe's, where I hope they'll stay till after supper," answered their mother. "Her kids have been here enough,

201

and I guess she can 'tend to mine for one meal."

"I can't go after 'em, 'cause I got to study my spellin'," announced Sophia.

"Nobody asked yer to," retorted Mrs. Bean. "They'd ought to know enough to come home alone."

The meal progressed to the accompaniment of jarring speech, and Polly was glad when it was over.

"Mamma, can we go up on the roof?" asked Katie. "The other folks are up there, and we'll keep away from the edge."

"I don't care; but, remember, the first one that goes near that rail gets a whippin'!"

The door slammed behind Maude, and Polly began to clear the table. She was taking up her old tasks as naturally as if she had never been free from them.

"Guess I'll go up myself for a few minutes," mused Mrs. Bean. "'Rastus, you go fetch Marcus and 'Melie home! Marcus 'u'd have a fit if we went up on the roof without him. And, Polly, you can put 'Melie to bed, and do up the dishes, and then come on up, if you want to. 'Rastus!"

The little man halted in the doorway.

"What, Jane?"

"Split up some kindlin's when you git back, and you may as well fix the fire for mornin' — it must be about out now."

The dishes were nearly washed when the children were brought in; and the boy had departed for the roof, and his small sister was in bed, by the time the new uncle had finished his chores.

"I'll put them plates up in the cupboard," volunteered the little man. "Set ri' down and rest."

But Polly helped, until the last dish was in place and the pan hung up on its nail. Then she dropped wearily into a chair.

"That Maude ought to have wiped 'em for yer," he sympathized. "But them kids!" He wagged his head soberly. "I'd ruther stan' at the bench, down to the shop, all day long, than be round with such actin' mortals. Jane, she can manage 'em if she sets out; but 'most gen'ally she don't set out. Wisht I could do somethin' for yer," he proffered. "Ye're all tuckered out!"

"Oh, I'm just a little tired — that's all!"

smiled Polly. "You are ever so good! I wanted to go up to the hospital, and tell them where I am — they don't know, and I'm afraid they'll worry! But I guess I can't to-night," she ended sadly.

"Why, I can run up there for yer, jus' 's well 's not," he nodded.

"Oh! will you?" she brightened. "I'll be so glad! But won't it be too much trouble?"

"Not a bit!" he returned glibly. Then his pinched face shaded. "If I can git back before she comes down," he hesitated, wavering between kindness and fear. "I guess I can," he decided, and put on his hat.

"If Dr. Dudley isn't there," Polly told him, "please ask for Miss Lucy Price. She'll do just as well. She's the nurse in our ward."

"I'll do it up all straight," he exulted, stepping briskly with the importance of his errand. But as his hand touched the knob, another's was before it. His wife opened the door.

"Where you goin', 'Rastus Bean?" she demanded.

"I — I was just goin' out for a little walk," he faltered.

"A walk!" she snapped. "If you've got yer chores done, you'd better walk into bed!"

Without a word he disappeared in an adjoining room, while his wife lifted the stove cover, to see if his tasks had been faithfully performed.

Polly's forlorn hope vanished with the little man; but no tears came until she was on her pillow, shut from all eyes. Then they gushed forth in a flood.

CHAPTER XIII

THE RETURN

POLLY was awakened early by clashing talk. The girls, whose room she shared, were in a wrangle over her pretty, blue hair ribbon.

Sophia had spied it first, and was slyly using it for her own straight locks, when Maude had snatched it away, and a hubbub followed.

The owner of it did not interfere, but began to dress, as if she had no interest in the cause of the quarrel.

"She's more stuck-up 'n she used to be!" Polly overheard Maude sneer, as she hurried away in response to her aunt's call.

Mr. Bean was already eating breakfast, and he greeted the little girl pleasantly, though keeping watch of his wife, who was frying cakes.

"Here! give these to your uncle," Polly was bidden; whereupon the little man began such attempts at kindliness as to draw out a contemptuous, "Huh!" from over the griddle. After that he fastened his eyes on his plate, and ate in silence.

By the time the elder children were off for school, and the younger had departed to a neighboring tenement, Polly's early tasks were completed, and she sat down again to the button-sewing.

The little kitchen was very still, and Polly's thoughts sped back to the big house on the hill. She wondered how long it would be before she should see Dr. Dudley and Miss Lucy. Were they worrying about her and trying to find her? She could only guess.

"I b'lieve I'll run up and get that gingerbread receipt of Mis' Moore's." The nasal voice broke in rudely upon the wondering.

Mrs. Bean shook the threads from her apron, and turned towards the door.

"If the kids come in and want something to eat, before I get back," she halted to say, "there's cookies in that little stone pot in the cupboard. Don't let 'em have but two apiece."

Wild thoughts, entirely foreign to Aunt

Jane's directions, were flashing through Polly's mind.

If only there were time! She could try it! She must let Dr. Dudley and the others know!

"I shan't be gone long," her aunt was saying. "You stick to your work!"

Polly waited only to hear her walk the length of the hall above, and a door open and shut. Then she cautiously stole out, and down the stairs, three long flights. Not more than a block away she had noticed a grocery. Groceries have telephones. She would run down there, and call up the hospital! At the outer door she paused an instant for one troubled look at her short skirt; but time was precious, and quickly she was speeding down the sidewalk.

"Hoh! look at her!" jeered a big boy from across the street.

She did not even glance his way.

"Have you a telephone?" was her breathless inquiry of a man at the entrance of the little shop.

A jerk of his fat thumb towards the dim interior was his only answer.

208

"Please, may I use it?"

He nodded indifferently, and then she was hurrying in the direction indicated.

The instrument was on the wall, and Polly on tiptoe could not reach the mouth-piece. Looking around for a possible foot-stool, she spied a small box, which might have been used before for a similar service, and pulling it into position she found that it brought her to the proper height. With a trembling hand she lifted the receiver from its hook. She was familiar with the hospital number, and gave it without hesitation.

"Put in your nickel!" came distinctly to her ear.

Polly started in dismay. This was a pay station!

"I — haven't any!" she faltered pathetically, and the merciless snap of the wire told her that her last hope had been cut off.

She pushed the box back where she had found it, and walked slowly out of the shop. Her feet still lagged when she turned towards the tenement. What mattered it if Aunt Jane should return and find her absent? What mattered anything now? Then came a

sudden daring temptation. The road was
free — and she was there! Why not keep on
to the hospital? She looked down — her
skirts were inches above her knees! If only
Aunt Jane had not insisted that she wear
Sophia's petticoats, to match the length of
the borrowed dress! Could she brave the
crowded streets in such attire? One thought
of those she loved best brought instant decision. She could dare anything for their
sakes. With a shrinking, fast-beating heart,
she turned, and went quickly forward.

She had not gone far, when ahead, whirling towards her, seemed a familiar object.
Could it be? There were other dark green
automobiles — but it was! — it was Dr.
Dudley!

Polly dashed into the road, — perilously
near the track of the approaching car, —
wildly waving her hands. It stopped almost at her feet, and then she was in Dr.
Dudley's arms.

For a moment she could only sob out her
joy.

"Where have you been, Polly, child? We
were all so worried —"

"I knew you would be! I knew it! But Aunt Jane made me come! She held me tight and I could n't get away! Mr. Bean was going to tell you last night; but she would n't let him — she sent him to bed! And I tried to telephone to you just now, and I had n't any five cents — oh, dear!"

"Poor little girl!" and the Doctor's voice was very tender.

His eyes passed beyond the curly head to the curb, where a knot of men and boys regarded them curiously.

"Where is the telephone, Polly?" he asked.

"Up there, in the little grocery store." Her hand showed the direction.

He swung her gently into the auto, stepped in beside her, and steered slowly towards the conspicuous sign.

"I'll be back in a minute," he told her, and disappeared between the shelves of fruit and vegetables.

Polly's eyes followed him lovingly. Presently he was beside her again.

"I wanted to let them know that you are safe," he smiled. "Now we will see that Aunt Jane."

They went up the long stairs, Polly in advance. Her aunt heard her, and opened the kitchen door.

"Where in the world —" she began sharply, but stopped at sight of the tall man.

"I did n't know anybody was with you," she muttered; and then recognized Dr. Dudley.

"I've had quite a hunt for you," he remarked. "You have moved recently."

"Yes," she assented, "when I was married; this is nearer his shop. I s'pose you're after Polly," she added; "but I've made up my mind not to let her stay at the hospital any longer. I need her at home."

"You will allow her to come to us for a day," he smiled, in a tone that admitted of no refusal.

"Ain't no need of her goin' back," she fretted; "I can send for her things."

"I'll agree to bring her luggage, when she comes for good," the Doctor returned pleasantly; "but we want her for another day or two, at the least. Polly, run and get ready! I shall be due at the hospital before long."

In the little dim bedroom the eager fingers

made quick work with the buttons. This was what Polly had not dared hope for, a day or two more with those she loved! Presently she was back in her pretty dress and shoes, and was fastening on her hat before the little cracked mirror. Oh, her locket! She had come near forgetting it.

"Please, Aunt Jane, can I have my locket and chain?" she asked, facing the somewhat disturbed woman.

"There's no call for you to wear it to-day," was the sullen reply.

"Oh, but I'd like it, please, if you don't mind!" Polly insisted, gaining courage from Dr. Dudley's presence.

With a toss of her head, Mrs. Bean stalked into the next room. The moments passed. Still she did not return. When she did appear, she looked actually troubled.

"That Gregory must have got hold of it, and gone and hid it away, or something!" she worried. "I've hunted high and low, but 't ain't anywhere! Now you need n't go to bein' scared, Polly!" for the little girl's face plainly showed her distress. "I guess you can stand it if you don't have on any *geegaws*

213

to-day! I'll get it fast enough when that kid comes home from school. But, oh, he's a terror, Gregory is!"

They went downstairs, Polly clinging to the Doctor's hand, as if she feared that even now something might separate her from him. In the auto, however, she settled back restfully in her seat. It was so unspeakably good to feel a loving protector close beside.

Dr. Dudley made quick time on the return trip to the hospital, and David was waiting for them by the stepping-stone.

"Hullo!" cried Polly blithely.

"Hullo!" he responded; adding, "Oh! what made you give us such a scare?"

"I could n't help it; truly I could n't!" she replied.

"Well, I'm glad you're back again!" David declared fervently, insisting on carrying her bundle and her little white sweater.

"Better run up to the ward, and let them have a sight of you," the Doctor advised. "Did you tell your uncle?" turning to the lad.

"Yes, sir. And I called up Mrs. Jocelyn, too; but she said she had just heard from you."

Polly's eyes grew wide and grave. Had her friends all been worrying like this?

Dr. Dudley glanced at his watch. "I shall be busy until noon," he said; "but, Polly, I wish you would come down directly after dinner. I want to talk with you."

She went upstairs wondering if the "talk" were to be about going back to Aunt Jane's. She had not reached any conclusion when the sight of Miss Lucy and Leonora put the troublesome matter from her mind.

"My precious!" breathed Miss Lucy in her ear.

"Oh, you darling Polly!" squealed the little lame girl, with a frantic hug. "We thought you must be kid — kid — kid-'aped, or whatever 't is!" she ended desperately.

"I was — by Aunt Jane," laughed Polly; "but Dr. Dudley rescued me."

"Maybe he would n't, if it had n't been for Colonel Gresham," returned Leonora, with a shake of her head, as the other children jostled her carelessly, in their eagerness to be at the front.

"What did the Colonel do?" queried

Polly wonderingly; but the rest claimed her, and the answer had to wait.

"You've lost your locket!" cried Stella Pope. "Did you know it?"

"It is n't lost exactly," Polly explained, instinctively shielding the guilty lad as much as possible in her brief narration of facts.

"Aw, what a kid!" sniffed Johnny Ryan.

"The horrid boy!" worried Mabel Camp. "What if they don't ever find it!"

"Where's yer hair ribbon?" asked Frederica, feeling responsible for the safety of that bit of dainty blue, since she had aided in its first use.

Again Polly stood in defense.

"My cousin Maude wore it to school, and she had n't come home when I left."

"What made yer let her?" mourned Frederica. "Bet yer I would n't!"

"Come, Polly, and change your dress," interposed Miss Lucy, guessing somewhat of the truth from the little girl's reddening cheeks and hesitating voice.

In the dressing-room, behind the closed door, the nurse took Polly in her arms.

216

"It is so good to have you back again," she told her, with kisses for emphasis.

The words stabbed the child's heart. The time was to be so short! Still Polly would not spoil to-day with to-morrow's or next day's troubles, and she summoned brave smiles and gay responses, until she half forgot the dreary fourth-floor flat where she had passed the night.

Leonora caught an early chance to draw Polly away to a corner where they could talk — or where she could, for she was bubbling with excitement over the untold story of last night's doings.

"My! I thought we'd go crazy when Mrs. Jocelyn telephoned to know why you did n't come! There you'd had time to get to her house over 'n' over again! Dr. Dudley just left ev'rything and went off in his auto, and hunted and hunted, and you was n't anywhere! Then he told the police, and they went to lookin'!"

"The police!" repeated Polly, big-eyed with astonishment.

"Yes; but they could n't find you. Miss Lucy 'most cried, and Dr. Dudley looked so

sober I did n't dare speak to him. Oh, it was
awful! We was sure you 'd been kid —"
Leonora hesitated, as before.

"Kidnaped," prompted Polly.

"Oh, yes, kidnaped! I never can remember how it goes. Well, David said he knew
you had been, and Miss Lucy kep' saying,
'Oh, no! it can't be!' But she looked as if
she 'd sink when she said it."

"And what was it about Colonel Gresham?" Polly asked. "You said —"

"Yes," Leonora hurried on, "I 'm comin'
to it! We never any of us thought of your
Aunt Jane, till Colonel Gresham he said
had n't you gone to see her. Dr. Dudley told
him of course you would n't, when you 'd
started for Mrs. Jocelyn's, and the Colonel he said he should try her anyway. So
Dr. Dudley jumped right into his auto and
raced off to where your aunt used to live.
When she was n't there, and the folks did n't
know where she 'd gone, and her name was n't
in the directory at any new place, he did n't
know *what* to do!"

"She 's married Mr. Bean," Polly put in,
"so she 's Mrs. Bean now."

"Oh, maybe that's why he could n't find her! Well, he come home, and he and Miss Lucy talked and talked, and High Price she talked, too, and —"

"High Price!" Polly broke out.

"Yes, she felt awful about your bein' lost — my! I guess we all did! You don't know! I did n't want to go to bed, and Miss Lucy let me sit up, hoping we'd hear something; but finally I had to, 'cause there was a woman sick, and the Doctor had to stop huntin' for you, and go and 'tend to her, and David went home, for there was n't anybody any more to telephone to. This morning Dr. Dudley he said he was going to find your Aunt Jane if she was in this city, and the next thing we knew David come rushin' in, and sayin' you was safe and sound — the Doctor had telephoned to him. My! how glad we were! I never wanted to dance so much in all my life! Say, why did n't you send word where you was?"

"I could n't." And Polly related something of her unhappy stay in the house on Chestnut Street.

She had not finished when David called

up to know if Polly and Leonora could be spared. He was alone in the office, and wanted them.

The lad was eager for Polly's story, and much of it had to be retold. Then he disclosed news of his own.

"We're going to move up to Uncle David's the first of next week. Won't that be jolly? You can come over any time; it is so near."

Leonora beamed her pleasure. Polly pushed back the tears.

David's face shaded with sudden dismay.

"You haven't got to go back to your Aunt Jane's?" he demanded fiercely.

Polly's head gave the answer. At the moment speech seemed impossible.

"You shall not!" he burst out. "If Dr. Dudley lets you go and live with those — those heathen, I'll never speak to him again as long as I live!"

"Why, David Collins!" Polly's gentle voice was grieved and full of astonishment.

The pale, blue-eyed lad seemed to have vanished, and another to be standing there before her. His eyes, grown suddenly dark,

220

set in that flaming face, gave him a most unnatural look.

"I shall have to go — Aunt Jane says I
must," she went on sadly. "There's no other
way."

"There would be another way, if I were a
man!" he raged. "Oh, oh! I wish I were! I
wish I were!" he cried passionately; and
throwing himself upon the couch, face down-
ward, his shoulders shook with sobs.

Leonora bent her head on her arm, and
wept silently.

Polly was endeavoring to soothe them
both when Dr. Dudley came in.

Learning the cause of the tears, he remon-
strated in his humorous way, until Leonora
smiled again; but David scorned such comfort, refusing to move or to speak. Finally
the Doctor started to prepare the medicine
he had come for, and the girls went upstairs,
Polly renewing her promise to return directly
after the noon meal.

CHAPTER XIV

DOCTOR DUDLEY'S office was without an occupant when Polly peeped in. The Doctor had not returned from dinner, and David had gone home for the rest of the day. The little girl wandered about the room, too full of vague dread to care for books, or even for the fine collection of sea shells, which usually she never tired of. They had been brought home from foreign shores by an old uncle of the physician's, and now, ranged on their wide shelves, they gleamed out from a farther corner of the office in all the delicate tints of their wonderful family.

But to-day Polly passed them by with only a sigh, remembering the happy times that she and David and Leonora had had in their close company, now playing that they were mermaids, come to tell them strange tales of the under-seas, now holding them to their ears, to catch the mysterious, fascinating songs of the ocean which they were always singing.

"Here already?" broke in the Doctor's pleasant voice. "I don't believe they gave you much of a dinner."

"Yes, it was good; but I was n't hungry this noon," Polly replied, with a wan little smile.

"You were in such a hurry to come down and see me that it took away your appetite — was that it?" he laughed.

"I don't know," was the sober answer.

The Doctor glanced furtively at her face, and grew grave at once. He squared some books and magazines upon the table, and then sat down in his lounging-chair, pulling Polly to his knee.

"I want to know more about that Aunt Jane of yours," he began. "Was your mother her sister, or —"

"Oh, no, she was n't!" Polly interrupted. "Mamma was an only child, just like me."

"And your father — did he have brothers or sisters?"

"I don't know," she answered slowly.

"He died when I was three years old. I can only just remember him."

"Do you recollect what Aunt Jane's name was before she married? Was it May?"

Polly shook her head doubtfully. "I can't seem to think," she mused. "Oh! I guess it was Carter, 'cause she's always saying that Maude is clear Carter, just like her folks, and Marcus is all Simpson, like Uncle Gregory."

"What was your mother's maiden name, her name when she was a girl?" the Doctor next questioned.

"Phebe Illingworth. Grandma Illingworth was her mother. She lived with us. She died the year before mamma did."

"Thistledown," went on the Doctor, "some of my questions may sound rude, but it is important that I know a little more than I ever have known of your family history. I think you told me that your mother gave piano lessons."

"Yes, and grandma gave lessons on the violin and guitar, and singing lessons too."

"And what became of the piano and other musical instruments?" asked the Doctor quickly.

"I think Aunt Jane sold them. She sold 'most everything. Some of the furniture she's got now."

"Was it nice furniture?"

"I think it was lovely. There was a beautiful sideboard — that was grandma's — with carved birds on it, and the wood was light brown — kind of yellowish — and so pretty!"

"Was that sold?"

Polly nodded sadly.

"Did your mother ever go to the bank, do you remember?"

"Oh, yes, she did! She used to carry a little book."

"Did you always have plenty of money to use — for food and clothes and so on?"

"I guess so. We had nice things to eat, and pretty things to wear."

"You never heard of any will, I suppose?"

The curls shook slowly.

"Your mother was not sick long, was she?" the Doctor asked gently.

"She was never sick. She was giving a music lesson, one afternoon, and she fainted away — they could n't make her live." The

225

sorrowful voice softened almost to a whisper, and the golden head drooped to Dr. Dudley's shoulder.

He touched his lips to the white forehead, and tightened his clasp of the slender little form.

"I am sorry enough to have to bring all this back," he said; "but, Thistledown, I must discover a way, if possible, to keep you from that woman. I want to find out just how much legal right she has in regard to you. If we could only obtain sufficient evidence to prove that she is not a proper person to care for you —"

Polly had suddenly sat up straight, her eyes round with the startling, beautiful thought.

"Do you mean," she broke in excitedly, "that I should n't have to go back to Aunt Jane?"

The Doctor bowed. "But —" he began.

"Oh, then I can stay with you!" she burst out. "She is n't proper, she is n't nice, she is n't — anything!"

"I know, my dear!" smiled the Doctor. "But such things are hard to prove. I shall

226

keep you, Thistledown, just as long as the law will let me; but the law must be obeyed, and we can't tell how things will come out."

"Won't I have to go back to-morrow?" she asked eagerly.

"No, indeed," he assured her. "Were you dreading that? Don't be afraid, Thistledown! Keep up a stout heart! You shall stay here for the present anyway." He looked at his watch. "I think I'll find Jack at home now," he said; and, letting Polly slip to her feet, he placed her in his chair and crossed over to the telephone.

Polly listened breathlessly. She knew that "Jack" must mean only Jack Brewster, a lawyer of the city, who had been a college classmate of the Doctor's. The two were close friends.

"That you, Jack?" Polly heard. "Yes. I want to see you professionally, as soon as possible. No," laughing; "but it is important. Can you come up this evening? All right. Good-bye."

"Jack Brewster will do his best for us," the Doctor said, coming back. "He says he will be here at seven or a little after. I think

227

it probable that he will wish to ask you a few questions; but you won't be afraid of him. He is one of the gentlest men I ever knew — and the strongest," he added.

"I am not afraid of anybody that is your friend," returned Polly.

The Doctor smiled. "A very pretty compliment!" he told her; but she gave his praise scant notice.

"I wonder," she said, "if you would like to see the little book mamma wrote about my Anne sisters."

"Your what?" he queried.

"My Anne sisters."

Only his twinkling eyes disclosed his amusement. "Ancestors you mean, don't you?" he corrected gently.

"Maybe," doubtfully; "but there are lots of Annes in it that are related to me."

"Where is the book?"

"Right upstairs, in 'Under the Lilacs.' Don't you remember, you went down to Aunt Jane's, and got some of my books when I was able to sit up?"

"I recollect," he nodded.

"Well, that was why I sent for this one

228

'specially, because I knew it had the little book in it, and mamma told me always to keep it. So I thought I'd better have it with me."

"Run up and get it, child! It may be —" Polly was gone.

It was indeed a very little book that she put in the Doctor's hand, simply a few sheets of small note paper sewed together.

"It has about the Illingworth family in one part, and about the May folks in the other," Polly explained; but it is to be doubted if Dr. Dudley heard her, so eagerly was he scanning those lists of names. He clutched at one forlorn thread of hope, and as he read, the feeble thread waxed into a cord of strength.

"Polly —" he began brightly, and then stopped. After all he could not be sure, and he must not raise happy anticipations only to see them blasted. His face shaded, and he finished the sentence quite differently from what he had intended. He went on gravely, "Did the Simpsons take charge of everything after your mother went? Was nobody else there?"

"Not to stay, except Mrs. Brooks, who lived downstairs. She was n't there much. I guess Aunt Jane did n't want her."

"Probably not," remarked the Doctor grimly.

"Is the book any good?" she asked wistfully.

Again he was tempted to tell her, and again he restrained himself.

"I think it will be of use to us," he replied.

"Did you see all the Annes?" she queried. "Are n't there a lot of them?"

He nodded laughingly. "It is a good name and I have discovered yours among them."

"Did n't you know it before? It is Mary Anne, after my great-aunt Mary Anne Illingworth. I don't like it so well as Polly."

"Or Thistledown," he added gayly. His spirits had risen wonderfully since seeing the little book.

The sudden change had its effect on Polly, and when she went upstairs it was with something of her accustomed blitheness.

The afternoon passed pleasantly, but after supper the little girl grew unaccountably nervous. She started at every ring of the telephone, and gave queer, absent-minded answers to Leonora's questions. Finally Miss Lucy, comprehending the situation, proposed a game; but Polly, usually the quickest of the children, allowed the others to eclipse her, while her ears were strained for the expected summons. At last, when the message came, she started downstairs with a fluttering heart, her nerves a-quiver with irrational fear.

At any other time she would have been pleased at thought of meeting Dr. Dudley's friend of whom she had heard so many delightful things; but now a vague terror possessed her, lest he, being a part of that awful law,—which to her was only a name of dread, — might send her directly back to Aunt Jane's.

Polly rarely had a fall, so light and sure of foot was she; but at the top of the flight she stumbled and came near going headlong. This, turning her thoughts suddenly into another path, seemed somewhat to steady her quaking nerves, and when she reached the office door she was ready to smile a brave, though shy, greeting to the lawyer.

Jack Brewster was in appearance the opposite of Dr. Dudley. The physician was tall and broad-shouldered, with no surplus flesh; yet none would have called him thin. The lawyer was slight almost as a boy, of fair complexion, with an abundance of wavy brown hair, and eyes that had a habit of shining as if their owner had just received a bit of good news. They shone now, as he took one of Polly's little hands in both his own, and told her how glad he was to make her acquaintance.

"I have n't any little girl at my house," he went on smilingly, "but there's a boy who makes things pretty lively. When I started to come away this evening he hugged my leg, and kept saying, 'No sir-ee-sir! no sir-ee-sir!' till I finally had to go back and tell him his usual bedtime story."

"How old is he?" asked Polly, her fears quite forgotten.

"He will be two years, the third of next month. Bob," whirling around to the Doctor, "why have n't you brought Miss Polly out to see us? I 'm ashamed of you!"

The physician laughed. "I am not very

neighborly, I'll admit," he returned. "Sick people have crowded out the well ones lately. I know well folks will keep."

"Then the only way for me to get hold of you is to feign a chill or a fever or a broken leg — all right! Thank you for the cue! And now, Miss Polly," he went on cheerily, "I want your honest opinion of that aunt of yours. Tell me, please, just how she makes you feel."

"Wh-y," hesitated the surprised little girl, "if I should say right out, I'm afraid it would n't sound very polite or —"

"Don't think anything about politeness just now, please. Open your heart frankly, and let me see what is there in regard to her. Don't be afraid to say exactly what you think. It may help me very much. I want to be able to look at her through your clear eyes."

A shadow darkened the fair little face, and pain crept in, and stayed.

"She seems," Polly began slowly, "like a dreadful dream — you know, when you wake up all shivery, and are so glad it is n't real. Only" — with a little catch — "Aunt

233

Jane is real! Sometimes I feel sick all over when I think about her, and going back there — oh," she burst out passionately, "I'd rather die than go back to live with her! Mr. Brewster, don't make me go! Please don't make me go!" The words came with a half sob, but she fought the tears back, and her appealing eyes searched his face for hope.

"My dear child," he exclaimed tenderly, "you must not worry one bit more about this! You have given me exactly what I want. Now leave the matter with Dr. Dudley and me. We will attend to Aunt Jane, and your part is only to forget her and to have a good time. Will you agree to do this?"

"If I can," she answered softly; "but Aunt Jane is very hard to forget!"

"I dare say she is," smiled the lawyer; "but I think you can do it. You know the best way to forget a disagreeable thing?"

No, Polly did not.

"It is to keep thinking of other things, pleasant things, until the mind is so full of them that there isn't a scrap of room for

234

whatever is annoying. You try it, and see if I am not right!"

"There are lots of pleasant things to think of," smiled Polly.

"To be sure there are! One is, that Dr. Dudley is going to bring you out to my house some morning to stay all day."

"Oh," beamed Polly, "that would be nice!" She looked across at the Doctor.

He nodded happily.

"If he does n't do it," and the lawyer made a comical grimace in Dr. Dudley's direction, "I'll come after you myself."

Polly gurgled out her little laugh, which sounded as if she had already begun to follow the lawyer's advice, and she thanked him very sweetly for his invitation and his promise. Presently she went upstairs, and Miss Lucy was relieved to see that she appeared more like her usual self. But she was very quiet, repeating nothing of what had passed in the office. It had been a hard day, and Polly was glad when the time came for her to creep into bed.

On Saturday Miss Lucy and her small assistant had a busy morning. There was

scant time to think about Aunt Jane. When
she did appear in Polly's mind, the little girl
remembered Mr. Brewster's counsel, and
hastened to perform her task in hand with
exceeding faithfulness, putting on fresh pillow slips with as much care as if the wel-
fare of the ward depended on their being
straight to a thread. Her efforts were suc-
cessful, too, for they pushed away Aunt
Jane. So the forenoon passed, leaving her at
dinner time a little more tired than usual,
but free from the worry of the day before.

Soon after the meal Miss Lucy went downstairs. When she came back Polly was playing Authors with Leonora, Mabel, Frederica,
and Stella. She stopped beside Polly's
chair.

"Dr. Dudley wants you," she smiled.
"Run right along, and I will take your
place."

Polly went, wondering, but fearing little.
Miss Lucy's face was too radiant to betoken
anything unpleasant.

Dr. Dudley held out his arms, and the
little girl ran into them.

"Glorious news, Thistledown! It is all

236

settled! 'Aunt Jane' has no right to you whatever!"

"Oh!" she gasped, and went suddenly white.

The Doctor dropped into a chair, and took her in his lap, letting her lean against him.

"I'm glad you are going to school next week," he declared. "You will get out of doors more. I'm not going to have you paling up in this way every little while. You are in the house too much."

"I'm all right," she argued. "Tell me about it, please!"

"To begin with," he smiled, "these people are no relatives of yours."

Polly's eyes rounded with amazement.

"And Aunt Jane isn't my aunt at all?"

"Not the least mite of an aunt," he laughed. "It was a hard thing for her to admit; but she had to do it."

"You have seen her?" queried Polly.

"Mr. Brewster and I were there this forenoon. It seems that she lived next door to you at the time your father died, and, according to her own statement, she gave your mother a great deal of assistance at that

237

time. It is easy to see how she made your mother feel under obligations to her, and the rest came about as it naturally might with such a woman. When she saw her chance for gain she improved it. She has defrauded you out of household goods and money; but Jack thinks we should hardly make anything by taking the matter into court. There is nearly two thousand dollars still to your credit in the bank, and that shall stay there till you are of age. She was allowed only a certain sum per week for your support — the rest she could not touch; but she did what she pleased, it seems, with the money received for furniture and so on. She has no property that we can get hold of, except the things which belonged to your mother. Those we can take, if you will tell me what they are."

"Oh! can I have mamma's little rosewood work-table! I saw it there the other day."

The Doctor was busy with pad and pencil.

"The sooner we get them the better, so think hard now, and I'll note them down."

"There's a good deal of china, and some nice glass dishes, and the silver spoons and

238

forks — I could tell which they were if I could see them."

"You are going to pick them out, with Mr. Brewster and me."

"I'm going there?" Polly cried.

Dr. Dudley nodded. "You're not afraid?" He smiled reassuringly.

"Oh, no, not with you!" she replied. "There's two trunks," she went on, "with some of mamma's clothes in. A good many are worn out — she wore 'em, and made 'em over for the girls and me. Then there are all our books, and three or four chairs, and a lovely clock — oh, and a great pile of mamma's music, with some pieces that she wrote herself!"

The list was longer than Dr. Dudley had expected. When Polly could think of nothing more, he called up the lawyer by telephone, making an appointment to meet him. Shortly afterwards he put Polly in the auto, and they started for Mrs. Bean's.

On the way the little girl thought of her precious locket.

"We shall get it if we can," the Doctor told her. "Mrs. Bean appears to be honest about that. She believes the boy has it; but he professes innocence. I fancy she will keep him out of our way if possible."

They took the lawyer in at his office, and Polly finished her ride sitting on his knee.

When Mrs. Bean learned their errand, she turned red, then white, and seemed greatly excited. At first she was inclined to resent their coming as an intrusion, declaring, "There ain't much belongin' to the kid anyhow." But, as earlier in the day, she quailed before Mr. Brewster's firm, quiet speech, and sullenly led the way to the various articles called for. Finally nothing remained unchecked on the list except the two trunks.

"I h'ain't got no trunks," the woman bristled. "You've seen my rooms an' all there is in 'em! Them trunks prob'ly was sold along with other things."

"Why, Aunt Jane," put in Polly, "they were here just before I was hurt. I remember, because —"

"Huh!" she cackled. "I wasn't here then, an' I guess they wa'n't!"

"I mean where we lived then," corrected Polly.

"Wal, they ain't here nor there now," she insisted.

"Can't we go up attic?" questioned Polly. "You said, the other day, there was an attic to —"

"I hain't got nothin' up there," Mrs. Bean broke in, with flaming face.

"Will you allow us to look through it, please?" The lawyer's voice was low, but tense.

"There ain't no call for you to go paradin' up there," she snapped. "Pretty how d' y' do, if you can't take my word for it!"

"It is an easy matter to be mistaken," Mr. Brewster smiled. "Have you a key to the apartment? Or is it open?"

Mrs. Bean took time for reply, narrowing her eyes, as if in deep thought. She was quick to see the loophole of escape which the lawyer had shown her. Still she hesitated.

"Wal," she muttered finally, "it's barely possible I was thinkin' o' some other trunks; but I don't b'lieve I was. I do' know; I'm driven to death. I sh'd think I'd forgit my own name, slavin' 's I have to! 'T won't do no hurt, I s'pose, for you to go up an' see."

The trunks were found, as Mr. Brewster had been sure they would be. He opened both, and he and Polly hastily looked over their contents. Besides bundles of old letters, photographs, and numerous little mementoes, there was much of value, — fine table and bed linen, a silk dress, some exquisite laces, and a little box of odd pieces of jewelry.

"Oh!" Polly burst out, "I forgot grandma's watch! And mamma's coral pin and her topaz ring!"

"They're downstairs," volunteered Mrs. Bean. "I forgot them, too!"

After the trunks were locked, and the keys in Mr. Brewster's pocket, he and the Doctor carried them into the hallway. While they were busy, there was a clatter of feet on the lower stairs, and Mrs. Bean slipped hurriedly away.

"I guess the children have come," said Polly.

But when the three reached the apartment below, no young folks were visible, and the lawyer silently concluded to defer his attempt with Gregory until another time.

An hour later Polly's goods were brought to the hospital, and Leonora and several other children, who were able to be downstairs, were given the unbounded delight of seeing them unloaded.

CHAPTER XV

A BID FOR POLLY

EARLY on Monday morning Polly received an urgent request from Mrs. Jocelyn that she begin her delayed visit that very hour. So, as school was to open on Wednesday, it was decided that the little girl should accept the renewed invitation, and that Dr. Dudley should fetch her home on the succeeding afternoon.

"By that time," observed David, "we shall be all moved, and we can go to school together in the morning."

"But, oh, dear!" groaned Leonora, "that Aunt Jane will get you again, sure! Oh, Dr. Dudley, don't let her go alone, please don't!"

Polly laughed happily. It was hard for Leonora to realize that Mrs. Bean had no more power over her beloved friend.

But Dr. Dudley did not laugh. Leonora had been of the band of anxious ones on that night of suspense, and he could understand how she still feared to have Polly venture far without a protector.

"You need not worry," he assured her. "I shall not let Polly out of my sight until she is safely inside Mrs. Jocelyn's house."

"I could go alone just as well," smiled the little girl. "There is n't any danger."

"It is too long a walk," returned the Doctor, "and don't you dare to come back, young lady, until you come with me!" He shook his finger at her threateningly.

She giggled, while David remarked, with a mischievous twinkle: —

"That would be a good way to keep her there — you need n't go after her!"

"Do you want me to stay away, David Collins?" demanded Polly.

"No, I don't," he admitted, laughing.

"Oh, don't talk about her staying away!" pleaded Leonora. "We did, just in fun, last time, and then she was lost!"

"Oh, you funny, blessed Leonora!" cried Polly, putting her arms around her friend's neck, "I'm not going to get lost, or stay away, either — only one night. I guess you can stand it for just one night."

Dr. Dudley saw his charge inside Mrs. Jocelyn's door, according to his promise; but the little lady told him that he need not come after her, for she would bring her back on the following day.

Mrs. Jocelyn's home was in a delightful quarter of the city, opposite a park of many acres. The house was a dignified mansion, full of stately old furniture, and if it had not been for its owner's cheery hospitality it would have been rather awe-inspiring to a little girl like Polly. But Polly, having been several times a guest in the big house, now felt quite at home, and ran up and down the polished oaken stairs and through the grand, dimly lighted hallways as merrily as if she had always been used to such imposing surroundings.

"It is too bad Dorothy could n't stay over till this week," Mrs. Jocelyn said; "but never mind! She'll come again before long, and then you'll see her. We'll have such pleasant times to-day and to-morrow, that she won't be missed. This afternoon we are going shopping, and you are to buy presents for everybody you like."

246

FORGETTING ALL BUT THE MUSIC SHE LOVED

"Oh!" beamed Polly.

"And to-morrow morning," her hostess went on, "we are invited to a musicale across the street, at Mrs. Trowbridge's, where we shall hear the wonderful little violinist who is being made so much of by musicians."

"Won't that be lovely!" cried Polly. "I have n't heard any music in ever so long, except at church, and David's singing."

Mrs. Jocelyn smiled appreciatively. "I knew you would enjoy it," she said. "Now I shall be busy for a few minutes, and you can do anything you choose, — mouse around the library, or play on the piano, or make out a list of what you 'd like to give your friends. We will start soon after luncheon. You won't have time for much; I 'm only going to make a salad dressing which I fancy I can mix a little better than Tilly can. Then I 'll help you with the presents."

Polly had taken lessons of her mother, and her fingers still remembered bits of the pieces she had learned; so the piano was her first choice. Lured on by the familiar airs, she played and played, forgetting all but the music she loved.

247

Mrs. Jocelyn returned from the kitchen, and, unnoticed, slipped into a seat back of the player.

Finally Polly turned around.

"I felt you there!" she laughed. "Have I hindered you?"

"You have been charming me. Why, child, I did n't know you could play so well! And all out of practice, too! I should n't think you could recollect a note."

"My fingers seem to," Polly smiled. "I 'll think I don't know a piece, and then my hands go right along and play it."

"I wish mine would," laughed Mrs. Jocelyn. "But I 've let my music go too long; it will never come back." Her last tones were a little sad, but she quickly recovered her gayety. "Suppose we think over now," she proposed, "what you would like to purchase at the stores, and where we shall need to go. Then we can the better map out our afternoon."

Polly was all eagerness at once, and her hostess was no less interested.

"Are n't there some new girls in the ward who have n't any dolls?"

248

"Yes," Polly answered, "there are five or six. Let me see," tapping off the names on her fingers, "there's Mabel, and Stella, and Frederica, and Angiola, and Trotty, — she's only four, — and Mary Pender, and Ida Regan, — she's real pretty; that makes seven: I think that's all."

"You shall choose a doll for each one of them. You will know better than I just what will suit."

"Oh, it will be such fun!" chuckled Polly. "And you are so good to do it!"

"Pshaw!" exclaimed the little lady. "I'm only being good to myself. I have just begun to learn what money is for, and I am enjoying it — for the first time in years!" A shadow stole over the wrinkled pink-and-white face; but a smile quickly chased it away. "Now, my love, whose name shall head your list of especial friends?"

"I don't know," Polly hesitated. "Do you mean children?"

"I mean anybody that you would like to honor with a gift. Suppose you begin with Miss Price — Miss Lucy Price."

"Oh, I'd love to! But what could I get?"

"Plenty of things to choose from, — books and jewelry and all sorts of knick-knacks, besides pretty bits to wear."

"I think she'd like a new hand bag," ventured Polly. "Hers is so gray and shabby. Would it cost too much?"

"No, indeed!" laughed Mrs. Jocelyn. "You shall buy the very prettiest one we can find. But before I forget it I must see about something else. I want your picture, and I know your hospital friends would like it, too. Wait a minute, and I'll call up Fisher, and secure an appointment for this afternoon if possible."

She disappeared in the tiny room back of the staircase, set apart for the telephone, and Polly heard her voice, as she talked over the wire. "I have promised to have you there at three o'clock," she announced presently. "That will give us a good two hours for shopping, if we don't talk too long over our luncheon."

"Am I dressed all right?" queried Polly, anxiously; adding, "Who will want my picture? The folks at the hospital see me all the time."

"Oh, you precious bit of humanity!" cried the little lady, taking Polly in her arms. "If I should tell you that you will make so sweet a picture that everybody will want it, would you believe it?"

"No," Polly laughed, "because it would n't be true."

Mrs. Jocelyn kissed her for answer, and then asked what she would like to give to David.

"He has a knife," mused Polly, scowling her forehead over the problem.

"How would a sterling silver fruit knife do?" suggested the little lady.

That was decided to be just the thing, and went down on the list. For Dr. Dudley, in addition to the photograph, Polly thought a nice handkerchief would be a suitable gift, and Mrs. Jocelyn wrote, "Box of H." opposite his name.

"Could I give Leonora Hewitt something to wear?" ventured Polly. "She thinks so much of pretty things; but she can't have many, because her father is poor, and there are a lot of children besides her. Leonora is a sweet girl — and, oh, is n't it lovely? Dr.

Dudley says now that she will get over her lameness, and be able to walk as well as anybody!"

"That is delightful!" agreed Mrs. Jocelyn. "You shall surely get a beautiful something for Leonora."

"Don't you think a pink hair ribbon would be nice?" Polly asked.

Her hostess smiled over the modesty of the gift, and was about to suggest some article of jewelry; but she finally let it go as Polly had chosen, only adding on the paper, "and sash."

"We may change every one of these, when we come to the real selection," laughed the little lady; "but the list will be a guide."

Nobody was forgotten, not even Miss Hortensia Price, an "Illustrated Browning" being against her name.

They were on their way shortly after one o'clock, in Mrs. Jocelyn's stately coach, drawn by the handsome iron-grays that were Polly's admiration. It would be hard to say which enjoyed the shopping most, Polly in her innocent delight of giving, or the old little lady who was fast growing young in her new-found life. With a carriage full of

252

bundles, they drove up to the photographer's precisely at the hour appointed, and Polly, radiant from her joyful experience, made a picture that charmed the artist as well as his patron.

The next morning's musicale was quite the feast that Polly had anticipated, and Mrs. Jocelyn's was a twofold enjoyment. The little girl had feared that her white dress was too wrinkled for so grand a party; so her hostess's maid had smoothed it into its original perfection, and, to make good the hair ribbon that had been lost, Mrs. Jocelyn had bought an even prettier one — the palest blue sprinkled with forget-me-nots, and sash to match.

After luncheon came the delightful task of giving the presents pretty holiday touches with fancy tissue papers and gay ribbons.

"We're having the best part of it, are n't we?" chuckled Polly, tilting her head to one side as she tied a pink baby ribbon around Leonora's dainty box.

The little lady did not instantly answer; then, dropping her work, she caught the surprised child in her arms with almost a sob.

"O Polly, Polly!" she cried passionately, "I must have you! I must! I must! You have taught me how to live, and you belong to me! O Polly! will you come?" She held her off, gazing pleadingly into her face.

"What — do you mean?" faltered the little girl.

"My darling! did I frighten you? I mean I want you for my own dear daughter! I have n't said anything before, because I feared the woman you have supposed was your aunt would not give you up. But now that you are free I feel that I must have you! I meant to speak to Dr. Dudley first; but I could n't wait, dearest! Don't you want to come and live with me? I know it's a gloomy old house, but I will make it all over into the sunshiniest home you ever saw. You shall have everything you wish! I will buy you the very prettiest pair of Shetland ponies I can find, and the loveliest little carriage! You can take your friends driving every day!"

"That would be beautiful," responded Polly, with a faint smile.

"And you shall have the nicest doll house

254

you ever heard of, and a whole set of furniture for your biggest doll! I'll fit you up two of the prettiest rooms in the house, and furnish them in white and blue! You shall have a new piano and take lessons of the very best master, and next summer we will go abroad and see all the wonders of Europe! Oh, there's no end to the happy things we'll do, if you will come and be my little girl! You will; won't you, Polly?"

"Why, I — don't know!" gasped the child. "You take my breath away!" She looked actually distressed.

"Poor darling!" The little lady folded Polly in her arms. "Of course you can't make up your mind all in a minute! I've thought of it so long, I didn't realize that it was news to you. I'm such an impatient body! Talk it over with Dr. Dudley, and he will make things all clear. Now we'll forget it, and finish up these packages. What do you suppose Leonora will say to her new ribbons?"

The voice was gay, so sure was the little lady that Polly, counseled by the far-seeing doctor, would make quick choice of so auspicious an offer.

But Polly could not easily be won back to her former blitheness. She finished her part of the task in an absent-minded manner; yet by the time she was on her way to deliver her presents she was more talkative and merry.

So splendid a coach was seldom seen on the poor, narrow street where Brida lived, and big-eyed babies and listless loungers watched its progress. Brida was at school; but her mother received with loud expressions of gratitude and praise the pretty doll carriage which Polly had brought.

Elsie, in a still narrower, dirtier street, had a similar gift; while for the others of Polly's hospital friends who had returned to their homes there were books and paper dolls, pocket knives and boxes of candy. It was a pleasant hour, yet Polly was not sorry when the carriage turned towards the hospital.

Mrs. Jocelyn would not go in, and the little girl bade her good-bye with a clinging embrace.

"I love you de-arly!" she whispered: which made the little lady smile happily to herself all the way up the street.

Nobody was in the Doctor's office, and

Polly lingered by the pile of packages which the footman had deposited on the couch. She was pulling out David's present from under the others, the present that had finally been changed from a fruit knife to a flute, when a voice from the doorway called out: —

"Hul-lo, Pol-lee!"

She turned, to see David's merry face.

"You can't guess what I've got for you!" chuckled the lad.

"You could n't possibly guess what I've got for you!" she retorted gayly.

David's eyes opened wonderingly, falling on the pile of bundles. Then he went back to his own secret.

Putting his hand in his pocket, he drew forth what Polly had feared she should never see again.

"My locket and chain!" she cried.

David grinned happily, and passed over the necklace.

"Where did you get it?" she questioned.

"You may thank Cornelius for it," he told her. "I met him down on Grant Street, and — I don't know what made me — I happened to speak of your losing this. He was

257

interested all at once, and wanted me to tell him just how it looked. When I said the locket was set with turquoises, he clapped his hand on his side and cried out, 'I bet yer that was it! I bet yer 't was!' It seems he'd seen a boy — only this morning — showing a locket to a little kid, and he thought then it was queer he should be having a girl's locket round that way. Cornelius said he could get it easy enough if the boy had it with him. So we went round to the school, and waited till 't was out. He had to go on an errand for his father this afternoon, and so was excused early.

"Burt Sehl is the boy's name, and Cornelius and I walked along with him till we got off the street — Cornel' was sharp enough not to tackle him near the school. As soon as the crowd thinned out, he asked him if he had that locket, and at first Burt put up a bluff. Finally he admitted that he got it from Greg. Simpson; said he swapped a lot of tops and marbles for it."

"I shouldn't suppose he'd have given it up," cried Polly excitedly.

David laughed. "He did n't without a

258

tussle; but Cornelius was more than a match for him — my! don't I wish I were as strong as he!"

"You will be some day," encouraged Polly. "But I'm glad I chose that book for Cornelius — it's all about a knight!"

"What book?" queried David.

"Oh, the book I left at his home for him this afternoon! I forgot," and she caught up the long parcel for David. "I hope you'll like that," she said.

The boy's eyes glistened when he saw what it was.

"Oh, you don't know how many times I've wished I had a flute!" he cried, fingering the little instrument delightedly.

"What's going on here?" called Dr. Dudley, from the open door.

"These are going *in here!*" flashed Polly, deftly transferring a square, thin package from the couch to the Doctor's pocket.

It caught and held by one corner, but the physician did not leave it long. He looked at it critically, and then laid it on the table, and began untying the bright ribbon which bound it.

259

"You have seen the hole in my Sunday handkerchief!" exclaimed the Doctor, dramatically, his eyes a-twinkle as he opened the box.

Polly and David laughed.

The handkerchiefs were fine and dainty enough to suit the most fastidious gentleman, and Dr. Dudley expressed sincere admiration for the gift.

Then the story of the locket had to be told again, and at its end David discovered that it was time for him to be at his new home.

Polly began to look over the packages, picking out what she wished to carry upstairs at once.

"Are n't you going to tell me about your visit?" asked the Doctor, dropping into his easiest chair with a luxurious sigh of relief, after a hard day.

The little girl's face grew suddenly grave. In the pleasure of the last hour she had forgotten the trouble that had been looming ahead of her ever since Mrs. Jocelyn's proposition. She laid Mabel's doll back on the pile, and came slowly over to the Doctor.

CHAPTER XVI

A SECRET

"YOU went shopping, I observe," began Dr. Dudley, tentatively.

"Yes," responded Polly, balancing herself on the arm of his chair. "Mrs. Jocelyn bought lots of things for me to give to people. We made out a list — or she did. She let me choose."

"That was kind."

"Yes," Polly assented, and then studied the rug for a moment.

The Doctor waited.

"We went to a musicale, this forenoon, at Mrs. Trowbridge's," she resumed. "The little boy was there who plays the violin so beautifully. Mrs. Jocelyn got me a new hair ribbon and sash to wear."

"Did you enjoy those better than the music?" twinkled the Doctor.

"Oh, no!" The tone was almost reproachful. "One piece the boy played was lovely.

I hated to have him stop. I wish I could play as well as he — no, I don't either! I don't want to!" she burst out fiercely.

Dr. Dudley glanced at her quizzically. "You seem to be a young lady of changeable opinions," he smiled.

Her lip quivered; but she struggled hard against tears.

"Suppose you tell me all about it, Thistledown," the Doctor said gently.

"Oh, don't let me go and be her little girl!" she broke out. "Don't! don't! I'll do anything, if you'll only let me stay with you!"

He drew her down into his lap, and soothed her with tender words.

"Nobody shall ever take you from me against your will, Thistledown!" His voice was tensely unnatural. "Does Mrs. Jocelyn wish to adopt you? Did she say so?"

"I don't know about adopting. She wants me to go and live with her. She said I could have everything, if I only would, — a new piano, and lessons, and two rooms all furnished beautiful, and a doll house, and go to Europe, and a pony — two of 'em — and, oh, I don't remember half!"

"And you are sure you wish to give up all that grandeur for this old codgery doctor who has n't any money?"

"You are n't old, and you are n't cod — the other thing — and I love you! Do you — do you want me to go?" she sobbed.

"Thistledown," — and his voice was very tender, — "I think such an arrangement as Mrs. Jocelyn proposes would break my heart. Still, if you really would be happy in going to her, I trust I should be unselfish and brave enough to give you up. But I am gladder than you can guess that you have chosen the life with me."

"I could n't choose any other way; but I love her, I love her ever so much!" Polly sighed. "I'm afraid she will feel bad not to have me go. Oh, I wish there did n't so many folks want me — first Aunt Jane, and now her!"

"It must be rather troublesome to be in such demand," the Doctor smiled.

"It is," responded Polly, between a laugh and a sob.

They sat for a while in silence, Polly's head nestled on the broad shoulder.

Finally Dr. Dudley spoke. "Can you keep a secret?"

"I think I could — I know I could," she answered slowly; "but I never have any to keep."

"I am going to let you into one," he smiled; "but you must n't breathe a word of it to anybody."

"Oh, I won't! I won't tell it as long as I live!" she declared solemnly.

He laughed. "This will not be so great a tax on your patience as all that. I hope the secret will be out in a month. Thistledown, what should you say if I should tell you that Miss Lucy and I are going to be married?"

Polly sat up straight, her eyes round with astonishment.

"Truly?" she cried.

"Truly!" he nodded.

"Why-ee! I never thought as you liked Miss Lucy very much! You acted just as if you liked High Price better!"

The Doctor's shoulders shook with soft laughter.

"And won't Miss Lucy be nurse up in the ward any more?" Polly queried.

264

"Not after we are married. We are going to housekeeping. You know the little brown cottage just beyond Colonel Gresham's?"

"The one with vines all over the piazzas?"

"Yes. That is to be our home."

Polly had dropped back on the Doctor's shoulder, and he, absorbed in his happy dreams, did not look down to note the shadow that suddenly swept all joy from the little face. When she spoke again, it was the tone rather than the words that brought him to himself with a pang of compunction.

"That — won't be so very far away," she faltered.

"Oh, Polly!" with a quick tightening clasp, "you did n't suppose we would leave you behind?"

She glanced up in sudden wonder and hope.

"Our home would n't be home without you. You are going with us, to be our own little daughter! We have it all planned; it has only awaited your sanction."

Polly lay very still, big teardrops trickling down her cheeks.

"You want to go, Thistledown?" the Doctor asked softly.

"Oh," she breathed, "I don't — dare — speak, for fear — it is n't real! It is so beautiful!" She stroked his big hand with her slender little fingers.

"It is very real," he smiled. "You need n't be afraid. We cannot give you the splendid things that you would have with Mrs. Jocelyn; but I can promise you all the love that any little girl could wish for. We want to make your life so happy that you will lose sight of the troublesome times that have gone before."

"I could n't help being happy with you and Miss Lucy." And Polly suddenly sprang up, flinging her arms around the Doctor's neck, and resting her cheek against his with almost a sob. "Oh, I wish mamma knew!" she whispered. "Do you s'pose she does?"

"We will surely hope so," he answered. "It seems to me that Heaven is nearer than some people believe."

"It would make her so happy," Polly went on. "I do wish you could have known mamma. She was such a dear!"

266

"I am glad to have so close a friendship with her little daughter," smiled the Doctor.

Light raps at the door made Polly slip to her feet, and sent Dr. Dudley across the room. Polly hurriedly brushed away the only remaining tear, and looked up to greet Miss Hortensia Price.

The nurse had come to talk with Dr. Dudley about a patient, and Polly went over to the couch, and searched among the parcels for a certain package. Her fingers trembled with joyous excitement. The world had suddenly turned rose color. Every sorrow had flown away. Even the grief which had been ever present with her for nearly three years was for the moment swallowed up in the joy of believing that mamma knew! She came upon the package she sought, examined it carefully to make sure that it was the right one, and then went, a little shyly, to Miss Price. She waited until Dr. Dudley stopped talking.

The lady received the holiday-attired parcel with a surprised look.

"Mrs. Jocelyn bought some presents," explained Polly, "for me to give to my friends, and I chose Robert Browning's 'Poems' for you. I hope you'll like it."

"Like it! Why, you dear child!" Miss Price dropped the book in her lap, and caught Polly's hands in hers. "How did you ever guess that Browning is my favorite poet?"

"You said so, one day, when we were playing Authors, up in the ward."

"And you remembered!" She began untying the ribbon. "I was thinking only yesterday that I must have a copy."

The volume was richly bound, and beautiful with illustrations. Miss Price fingered it with the caressing touch of a booklover. If her thanks were a bit conventional, Polly knew that back of them lay real gratitude and appreciation.

The little girl went back to her parcels with an added gladness. She began piling them on her arm.

"Don't carry too many," warned Dr. Dudley. "I'll take them up for you."

"I will bring some along when I come," promised Miss Price.

So Polly put back all but two dolls and a

few small packages, and started upstairs humming softly a gay little air.

Presently the song was hushed by happy thoughts. To think of living in a dear little cottage, all alone with Miss Lucy and Dr. Dudley! To sit down at the table, three times a day, with them both! And at bedtime! There was never room for jealousy in Polly's heart; but sometimes when Miss Lucy cuddled the littlest ones in her arms, her mother-hungry soul felt starved out of its rightful food. And now! — she could almost feel the dear arms around her! She stopped halfway up the second flight, and bent her head reverently.

"O Lord Jesus, I thank thee!" she whispered. "Please let mamma know how beautiful it is going to be! For Thy Name's sake. Amen."

The door of the ward was open; but so light were her footfalls that she stood on the threshold a moment before being noticed. Then came a shout and a rush and such frantic huggings that Polly and her parcels seemed in danger of coming to sorrow.

"That is for Stella," Polly finally managed

269

to say, freeing a hand long enough to pass the box over one or two heads to the little girl beyond.

This turned the attention in Stella Pope's direction, and Polly hastened down the room to a cot where a little girl lay, her big blue eyes staring out in line with her pillow, taking no note of the commotion going on behind her.

"Trotty, see what I've brought you!" was Polly's cheery greeting.

The little four-year-old turned slightly, with a wavering smile. She was a strange wisp of a girl, and Polly was not in the least disappointed when she made no answer, only watched the fingers that were untying the bright ribbon.

"Now — what do you s'pose?" smiled Polly, staying the cover a moment to make the gift of more effect.

There was a look of expectancy on the midget's face. A word of joy broke from her lips.

Polly laid the beautiful doll in her arms, smiling to see the rapture in the big blue eyes.

Then a wee shadow crept over. "Mine? All mine?" questioned the tiny one.

"Yes, all yours," was the sure answer. "Isn't it a darling?"

Trotty did not speak, but hugged the new baby to her heart in a way that left no doubt. Polly wished that Mrs. Jocelyn were there to see.

After the other smaller packages had been left with the several patients for whom they were marked, Polly said, in a voice that carried to all the cots: —

"This isn't all. There is something for everybody; but I couldn't bring so many. Dr. Dudley and Miss Price are coming up with the rest."

That started a babel of joyous questioning; but Polly was responsive and patient, and altogether so satisfactory, that the little sick people settled back on their pillows in supreme content, to await the coming of their presents.

The others had heard, too, and pressed about Polly with eager talk.

"I chose a doll for every girl that hasn't any," she told them gayly, "and I got

271

just as pretty ones as there were in the store."

"Say, what colored hair has mine?" questioned Mabel.

"Light, like Stella's, I think."

"Oh, goody!" squealed the little maid. "And is it curly?"

Polly nodded.

"Wha' d' yer buy for Leonora?" queried a curious one.

Polly threw a bright smile across to her friend, while she answered merrily: —

"You wait! It's something pretty."

"I guess Polly's had an awful good time," observed thoughtful Mary Pender; "she's so full of fun."

Miss Lucy, entering the ward at the moment, overheard the remark, as her eyes met Polly's.

The little girl waived a reply, and ran over to greet the nurse.

"Is Mary right?" Miss Lucy smiled.

Polly hesitated, growing grave. Then her eyes danced mischievously. "Just about right," she answered softly. "It was 'good' and 'awful' both. But I had a lovely time

272

with Dr. Dudley after I came home —
lovely!"

Miss Lucy sent a quick searching glance
into the happy eyes, and they fell before it.
Polly feared she had told too much. But no,
she reasoned, because the secret was also
Miss Lucy's. She looked up again half
shyly. The nurse's cheeks were very pink,
and her lips were smiling.

"Precious child!" she murmured; and
then she kissed her, a bit of favoritism which
she seldom allowed herself. But there was
now an excuse. Polly had been away.

Shortly afterwards Miss Hortensia Price
and the Doctor appeared, laden with happiness for the ward. The dignified nurse
seemed in a holiday mood, to match her be-
ribboned armful, and she remained to see the
delight of the children, as they unwrapped
their presents.

Leonora lingered over the untying of her
box, as if reluctant to risk the pretty flowered
bit of pasteboard for what lay within. Polly
went across to where she sat.

"I'm waiting to know how you like it,"
she smiled.

Leonora finally lifted the cover, and her long-drawn, "O-h!" of surprise and joy was enough for the donor.

"It is just like mine," Polly explained, "only mine is forget-me-nots on pale blue."

"That must be lovely," said Leonora; "but I like this best for me — it don't seem as if it could be for me!"

She carefully raised an end of the broad white sash ribbon, and sighed rapturously over the beautiful pink rosebuds scattered along its length.

"That is exquisite," agreed Miss Price, coming to her side. "Pink is exactly the color for you. Polly has shown excellent taste in its selection."

"Oh, Polly always knows just what's right!" praised Leonora.

Miss Price did not reply, only smiled across to Polly in the friendliest way.

"Is n't High Price lovely this afternoon!" whispered the lame girl, as the tall nurse turned to admire a doll which was held up for her inspection.

Polly nodded happily. Everything was

"lovely" now. What a glad, beautiful world it was!

"My dear!" A pair of soft arms clasped her from behind, and Polly found herself looking up into Miss Lucy's radiant face. "I believe you are a little witch!" she laughed. "You have given me just such a bag as I have coveted for a good many years, but which I never expected to own."

"I'm so glad!" responded Polly. "But Mrs. Jocelyn chose it — the kind, I mean."

She might have added that she should never have dared select one at that price; but she only smiled joyously.

"Then I will thank you and Mrs. Jocelyn both," smiled Miss Lucy, moving away with the other nurse.

"Wasn't it nice of her to buy all these things for you to give to us!" said Leonora happily.

Polly's response was sober. She could not quite forget how sorry the dear little lady would be when she heard what had been decided. But her seriousness soon gave place to laughter. The ward was in too merry a mood to allow aught but mirth within its walls.

CHAPTER XVII

THE WEDDING

THE next morning David called for Polly on his way to school, and the two went off together, the children waving good-byes from the windows. They returned, at noon, in love with their teachers, in love with the scholars, in love with their new books and all pertaining to the school. Such funny, interesting things had happened, and Polly told about them all dinner time.

Leonora watched her two friends go back in the afternoon, feeling a little sad. If only she could go, too! But she was growing well and strong; Dr. Dudley had assured her that she would soon be able to run about like other girls. The sadness, after all, ended in a long breath of joy.

The weeks before the secret came out were very happy weeks for Polly. Only a few days after her visit to Mrs. Jocelyn came a package, a large, flat, nearly square package. It

arrived while she was at school, and she
found the children eyeing it curiously as it
lay on Miss Lucy's desk.

"It's for you," announced Stella, "and she
said there mustn't anybody touch it. She
wouldn't open it herself."

Polly looked at the white parcel, and wondered, too. She had been expecting the
photographs; but this was too big for those,
she decided. Hastily she untied the string.
Miss Lucy came in just as she turned back
the wrapper.

"O-h!"

"Why, Polly May, you've gone and had
your picture taken!"

"My! ain't it splendid?"

"Whew! bet that cost somethin'!"

Miss Lucy caught a glimpse of the photograph, which brought her quickly across the
room.

"Polly dear, what a surprise this is!"

"I don't think it looks much like me,"
murmured the little girl, staring wonderingly at the beautiful picture.

It was of large size, exquisitely finished in
carbon, and mounted in a handsome folder.

"Why, it looks exactly like her! Don't it, Miss Lucy?" queried Mabel.

"I think I never saw a better likeness," smiled the nurse.

"There!" exulted Mabel. "Say, what made you think it did n't?"

But Polly only laughed a little uncertainly. "Never mind, if you like it!" she told them.

"Oh, here's another kind!" piped Stella, whose curious fingers had discovered a photograph showing Polly in a different pose.

This was full-length; the other was only head and shoulders.

"There's one more, I think," said Polly, "where I had some flowers in my hand."

A hunt soon revealed it, — "the very sweetest of all!" Leonora declared.

The girls hung over it rapturously.

"Will you give me one?" begged Mabel.

"And me?" — "And me?" — "And me?" chorused the others.

"Polly cannot tell right off just what she will be able to do," interposed Miss Lucy. "Dr. Dudley has n't seen them yet. Suppose

you run down and show them to him,
Polly."

Down the stairs skipped Polly, glad to get
away from the too eager children.

The Doctor received them delightedly.
Polly watched him with thoughtful eyes.

"Do you think they look like me?" she
ventured at last.

"Very much," he answered, smiling at the
anxious pucker between Polly's eyebrows.
"What is the trouble?"

The pink in her cheeks deepened to crim-
son. "I am not — so pretty as that," she
faltered. "You know I'm not. And I hate
to give away such pictures. It seems as if
folks would think I wanted to make out I
looked better than I really do."

Dr. Dudley's eyes were bent to the photograph in hand. He thought hard and fast.
Should he tell her the truth, — that the
beautiful black-and-white print, with all its
exquisite softness, scarcely did justice to the
delicate mobile face?

"I wanted you and Miss Lucy to have
one," she went on, "and Colonel Gresham,
and David, and High Price, and Leonora,

279

and Cornelius — for he was so good to get my locket back. Then the rest of them — there are a dozen — I thought I'd give to anybody that wanted one; but now —" she halted appealingly.

"Well, if I were you, Thistledown," and the Doctor threw his arm in a comradely way across the slim shoulders, "I should go straight along and give my pictures to those for whom I had intended them, with no thought about any lack of resemblance. You sat for the photographs, and you are not to blame for any possible mistake the camera may have made; so don't let it bother you."

She gave a little gleeful chuckle. "It is the camera's fault, is n't it? I never thought of that. Well, if you think it's all right to give them away, it must be; but it did n't seem quite — honest, you know." She looked up, still a bit anxious.

The Doctor smoothed away the tiny wrinkle on her forehead, and smiled down into the clear brown eyes.

"It is perfectly right, Polly; in fact, it would be wrong to spoil so much pleasure for such a little reason. The pictures are far more lifelike than most people's are, and nobody will stop to compare them with the original, feature by feature."

"No, I guess they won't," she laughed. "You pick out the one you want to keep, and next I'll let Miss Lucy choose."

Dr. Dudley watched her, as she danced away happily up the stairs. Then he studied the photograph before him, doing exactly what he had assured her that no one would think of doing; but his final judgment, like his first intuition, was not in favor of the print.

The simplest of church weddings had been planned by the two most closely concerned, for neither had other home than the hospital; but Mrs. Jocelyn overthrew plans and arguments together.

"What is my big house good for," she demanded, "if it cannot be useful at a time like this? You shall come and make it merry once more in its old life!"

She ended by carrying off Miss Lucy for a whole week before the appointed day, and the hospital had to hustle another nurse into the ward which was both sorrowful and glad.

That was a week of happy upsetting for the stately old mansion. Carpenters, electricians, florists, and tradespeople of various classes, all joined in the joyous whirl. Dr. Dudley and Polly whizzed back and forth in the automobile, and the dignified grays were kept trotting to and from the house at all hours of the day and evening.

It had been early arranged for Polly and Leonora to remain with Mrs. Jocelyn for the two weeks that the Doctor and his wife were to be away on their wedding journey, and the little lame girl, who now had only the tiniest limp, was in alternate rapture and dismay.

"To think," she would exclaim, squeezing Polly ecstatically, "of *me* being in that splendid house, with you and that beautiful Mrs. Jocelyn for fourteen whole days! But, oh, mercy!" she would cry, "I'm dreadfully afraid she'll not want me so long! I shall be sure to say or do something wrong! I'm not used to grand folks like her;" and the joy would end with a sigh.

Then it was Polly's part to reassure her with laughing words, until the delight would come back to crowd out all fears.

282

One large room in the house on Edgewood Avenue had been reserved for the wedding presents, and, although Miss Lucy had jestingly remarked that a little hall chamber was more than would be needed, the apartment was packed with love tokens long in advance of the day. Both the nurse and the physician had won many friends in their years of hospital service, and now all seemed anxious to show honor to these two who had helped to add length and comfort to their lives.

One morning, just before starting for Mrs. Jocelyn's, Dr. Dudley read this note to Polly: —

MY DEAR DOCTOR, —

I have been wondering, ever since I heard your good news, how Polly was going to ride, inasmuch as two fill your runabout. I have too much consideration for the lady who will sit by your side to wish her always to bear the burden of Polly's weight; so I have ordered for you a car that will seat five without crowding. There is a place ready for it in my carriage house. That won't be far for you to

283

come, and it will be handier for me whenever Lone Star goes lame.

Your sincere friend,

GRESHAM.

Lucky for me I happened to think of this, for it would get on my nerves to see Polly hanging on behind every time you and Mrs. Dudley went to ride.

D. G.

"What a funny man!" laughed Polly. "You'd think Lone Star went lame about once a week! But is n't that a lovelicious present — a big auto! — my!"

"It is too much." Dr. Dudley shook his head gravely.

"Why, he loves to do it for you," argued Polly. "Besides, it is not just for you," she chuckled; "it is so he won't have to see me sitting in Miss Lucy's lap or 'hanging on behind'! Would n't that look funny?"

The Doctor laughed, and put the note in his pocket.

At Mrs. Jocelyn's, Miss Lucy met them at the entrance.

"I'm so glad you've come," she cried. "I

was wishing you would, to see what Colonel Gresham has sent me."

"Why —" began Polly, and then stopped, blushing at having almost told about the new motor car. That was not hers to speak of first.

Dr. Dudley sent a swift glance of appreciation in her direction, and followed Miss Lucy's leading.

"That came for you, Polly, at the same time," she said, handing the little girl a small square package. "A man just brought them."

"For me?" Polly's eyes opened wide. "I'm not going to be married!"

They laughed, while the young lady displayed her gift, a necklace of pearls.

"Oh, is n't that lovely!" exclaimed Polly. "How sweet you will look in it! Do put it on!"

But Miss Lucy declared that pearls and gingham dresses were not companionable, and the necklace was returned to its satin case.

"Why don't you undo your package?" inquired Mrs. Jocelyn.

285

"Oh, I forgot!" cried Polly, in sudden compunction. "Those beautiful pearls put everything out of my head."

She soon had the wrappings off, disclosing a small leather case.

"What can it be?" she breathed. "Oh, you darling!" gazing delightedly at an exquisite little watch. She caressed it with excited fingers. "Why, there's something engraved in here!" as the case flew open, and, turning to the light, she read aloud: —

To Polly of the Hospital Staff, in remembrance of a stormy midnight and a sunshiny morning, from her devoted lover, DAVID GRESHAM.

"And here's something more," she went on, scowling in a puzzled way over the quotation. "It says, 'Blessed are the peacemakers.' I don't see what that's for, do you?"

The others smiled comprehendingly.

"Why, dearest," explained Mrs. Jocelyn, "you know you brought the Colonel and his niece together."

"Oh, no, I did n't do it!" protested Polly.

286

"I wonder who did," the little lady laughed.

Miss Lucy was reading the Colonel's note, which Dr. Dudley had given her. She ended it with a silent chuckle, and the Doctor passed it over to Mrs. Jocelyn.

"Just like David!" the little lady declared. "He enjoys a bit of quiet fun as well as any man I ever knew."

Polly had gone back to her present, hanging over it in delight.

"It is just the right kind of watch for a little girl like you," admired the Doctor; "neither too large nor too ornamental."

"It is beautiful!" sighed Polly rapturously. "Isn't Colonel Gresham nice to give it to me?"

The Doctor smiled an emphatic "Yes," which rejoiced Polly's heart. She had been afraid he would shake his head, as he had shaken it over the touring-car. In that case, she reasoned conscientiously, she should have felt as if she ought to give back her watch.

It was a six-o'clock wedding. The bridal procession formed at the foot of the stairs in

287

the spacious hallway, marching its length, and then proceeding through the east drawing-room to the library, where the ceremony took place under a canopy of roses. A troop of children attended the bride, children to whom, as nurse of the convalescent ward, she had at some time ministered. The girls, two and two, gowned in silken chiffon of harmonious colors, had each a basket heaped with blossoms. Polly and Leonora came last of all, both in delicate pink, from the ribbons that bound their hair to the tips of their kid slippers, Leonora's black braids in happy contrast with Polly's fair curls. The boys, clad as pages, ranged, at regular intervals, on either side of the long line, carried light arches of vines and flowers, making a fragrant arbor for the others to walk under.

The brief service over, the flower girls strewed roses in the path of the bridal pair all the way to the great west drawing-room.

It was like a queen's pageant in a vision of fairyland. The myriad lights, the gayly dressed children, the lavish profusion of

THIS DOCUMENT MAKES YOU LEGALLY OUR OWN DAUGHTER

flowers, the soft music floating from a bank
of ferns, — all united to make the scene unusually dreamlike and beautiful.

As the bride stood to receive her guests, in
her simple white silk gown, the necklace of
pearls her only ornament, Polly gazed into
her sweet, thoughtful face, and longed to
throw her arms around her neck and give her
a loving hug. But she had to be content with
only one little decorous kiss, and she con-
soled herself with the words that had been
singing in her heart all the day, "She is going
to be my mother! She is going to be my
mother!"

There were many guests, and it was long
before the bride and groom were free from
hand-shaking. Polly only caught glimpses
now and then of the two she loved best. She
was with a group of merry children, when she
heard her name softly called. Turning, she
saw Dr. Dudley in the doorway. She ran to
him, and he led her into the library, where
his bride was talking with Mr. Brewster,
the lawyer.

Mrs. Dudley drew her down beside her on
the divan, and Mr. Brewster soon took leave

of them. The Doctor seated himself on her right.

"This document," he smiled, tapping lightly the paper in his hand, "makes you legally our own daughter. We have just signed it, for we wanted everything settled before going away."

With a quick, graceful gesture, Polly wound an arm around each neck.

"My dear new father and mother," she whispered solemnly, as if it were a prayer, "I will be just as good, always, as I know how to be, so you won't ever be sorry you made me your own little girl!"

THE END

The Riverside Press
CAMBRIDGE · MASSACHUSETTS
U · S · A

MOTHER CAREY'S CHICKENS

By KATE DOUGLAS WIGGIN

"A fitting successor to the far-famed Rebecca."
Boston Transcript.

"Mother Carey is one of the sweetest and truest models of motherhood imaginable." *The Outlook.*

"A book to enjoy, a book to love, and a book to be grateful for." *Westminster Gazette.*

"A delightful book for girls, not to mention the boys and the mothers and fathers, is 'Mother Carey's Chickens,' one of the best of the many good stories that Mrs. Wiggin has written. . . . Mother Carey is a real human mother and her children are a lively flock of real youngsters, all different and all worth knowing." *Springfield Republican.*

"A book to brighten and sweeten every home into which it enters." *British Weekly.*

Illustrated in color by Alice Barber Stephens.
12mo. **$1.25** *net.* Postpaid, $1.36

HOUGHTON
MIFFLIN
COMPANY

BOSTON
AND
NEW YORK